Advance Praise for *So Twines the Grape*

"First-time novelist Cavill Greeves-Dunn takes what we are all thinking, that the South is the decaying embodiment of the cataclysms of a dying culture, and places it in an unforgettable landscape of rotten tree trunks, starry cricket-filled nights and various kinds of interesting moss. *So Twines the Grape* twines in fact around nothing less than the all-too-fragile human heart itself. A touch of this 'Grape' will do you good!"

— Edna Boor, author of *The Old Stump, Got My Toe Caught in the Bucket* and *Uncle Fussy is Dead*

"A stunning achievement.... *Grape* is nothing less than a white-hot Southern pitchfork rammed up the virginal ass of literature by a grinning gap-toothed demon in a straw hat and overalls, crawling with pellagra and ringworm and about to faint in a primitive ecstasy of religious zeal. Greeves-Dunn uses the tractor of her talent to plow the fallow Southern fields of genius, uncovering the cracked bones of truth and planting the seeds of a fiery enema for the soul."

— Scoop Taylor, author of *Granny's Storebought Chompers: A Picaresque*

"*So Twines the Grape* combines heart-stopping suspense, jaw-dropping plot twists and bowel-emptying shocks with spleen-ripping style, skull-pulping characterizations and spine-crushing lyricism. I am not given to hyperbole, so believe me when I say that reading this book will make your head pop off and roll around the room. Then your head will come back up on your neck, but it will be facing the wrong way and there won't be a thing you can do about it. Nor will you want to, thanks to this page-turning charmer!"

— Johannes Coddle, author of *The Philatelist's Nephew*

More Advance Praise for *So Twines the Grape*

"One sentence made me vomit with excitement. Another made me scream with pity. My only advice is to read it for yourself and see what happens to you."

— Hurly Jo Perch, author of *The Inspector's Last Muffin* and *Lightly Boils the Dumpling*

"In this genre-busting masterpiece of Americana, Greeves-Dunn treads ground where few writers have dared to go before. Sophocles, probably. Shakespeare, almost certainly. Goethe? In his dreams! To call *So Twines the Grape* a book is like calling the Crucifixion a minor scrape.... Reads like an unholy amalgam of Oscar Wilde, Harold Robbins, and some writer that will never be born. You have never read anything like it. After you read it you should blind yourself so that lesser works cannot offend your eyes. I know I did."

— Winston Fist, author of *Skippin' Skool* and *Still Skippin'!*

"I killed my entire family after reading *So Twines the Grape.* It was for their own good. How could they compete with the glory of this fine first novel, which finds its only competition for true importance in the Unblinking Face of God Himself? Now I'm headed to the shopping mall to wreak Holy Justice on a nation of sheep who do not deserve a book like this. Then I will turn the gun on myself. Thank you, Cavill Greeves-Dunn, for reminding us what literature is all about."

— Hogan Dump, author of *Frisking the Pig*

THE MYSTERIOUS SECRET OF THE VALUABLE TREASURE

STORIES BY JACK PENDARVIS

THE MYSTERIOUS SECRET OF THE VALUABLE TREASURE

STORIES BY JACK PENDARVIS

MacAdam/Cage

MacAdam/Cage
155 Sansome Street, Suite 550
San Francisco, CA 94104
www.macadamcage.com

Library of Congress Cataloging-in-Publication Data

Pendarvis, Jack, 1963-
The mysterious secret of the valuable treasure : stories / by Jack Pendarvis.
p. cm.
ISBN 1-59692-128-5 (hardcover : alk. paper)
I. Title.
PS3616.E535M97 2005
813'.6--dc22

2005017986

Manufactured in the United States of America.
10 9 8 7 6 5 4 3 2 1

Book and cover design by Dorothy Carico Smith.

Some of the stories in this collection were previously published elsewhere: "Attention Johnny America! Please Read!" in the anthology *Stories From the Blue Moon Café III* (MacAdam/Cage, 2004); "Dear *People* Magazine, Keep Up the Great Cyclops Coverage" in *McSweeney's Internet Tendency*; "The Golden Pineapples" in *Fourteen Hills*; "Our Spring Catalog" in *Chelsea* and the *Pushcart Anthology XXX* (W.W. Norton, 2005); "The Poet I Know" in *Yalobusha Review* and the anthology *Alumni Grill II* (MacAdam/Cage, 2005); "Sex Devil" in *The Ruminator*.

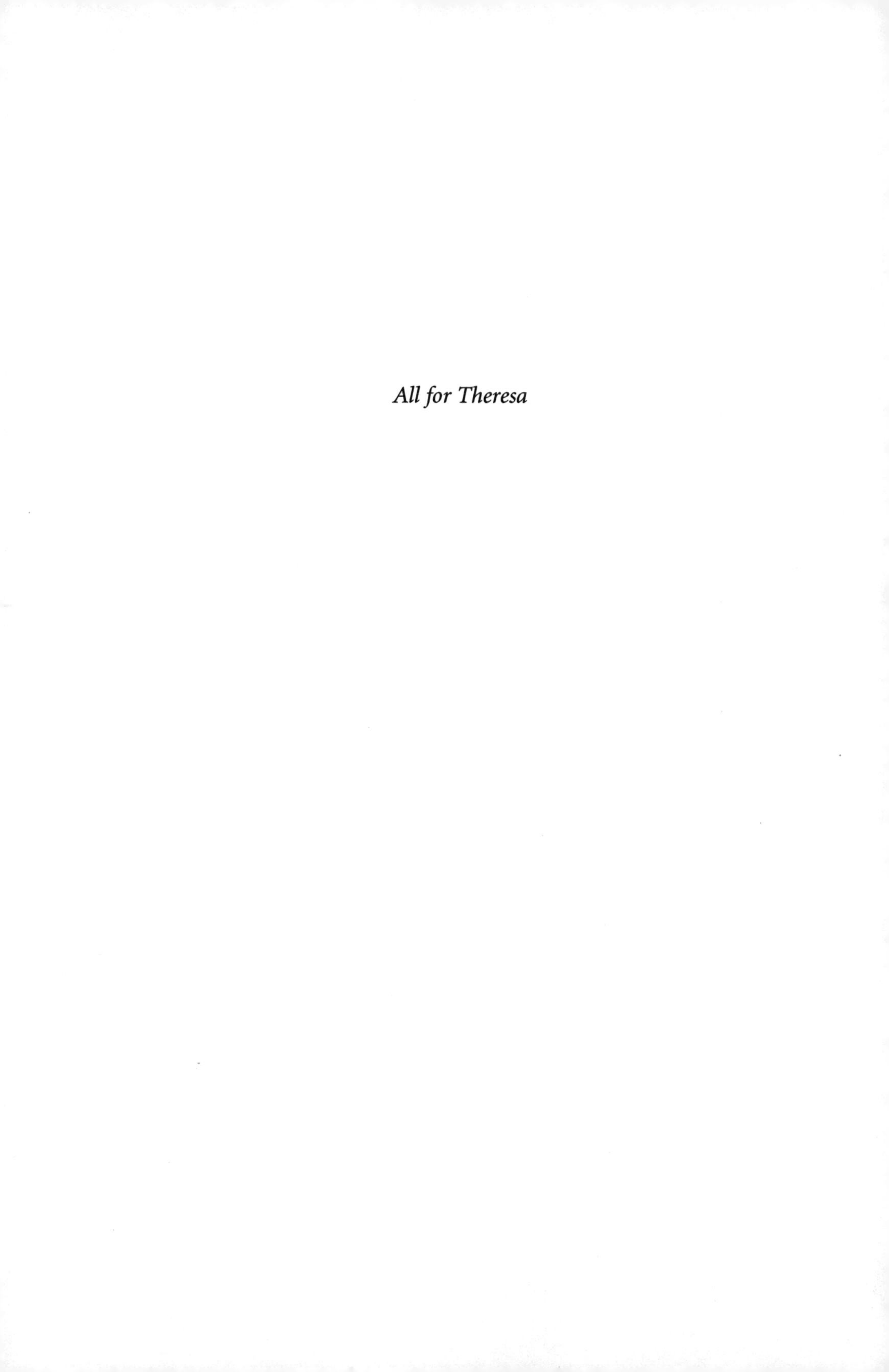

All for Theresa

TABLE OF CONTENTS

Diseases and pests were a constant threat. Wolves and wildcats from the mountains killed sheep, rodents attacked chickens, rattlesnakes and copperheads were a danger, and there were crows, potato bugs, many mosquitoes, and occasionally a demented cow.

—*From Pioneer Settlement to Suburb: A History of Mahwah, New Jersey, 1700-1976*
by Henry Bischoff and Mitchell Kahn

Das ist deine Welt! Das heißt eine Welt! —*Faust*

SEX DEVIL

Gentlemen:

I would like to give you my idea for one of your comic books. Well it is not one of your comic books yet, but it soon will be! I call my idea Sex Devil.

Sex Devil starts out as a normal high school student. Unfortunately his fellow classmates do not think he is normal. For you see, Sex Devil (real name Randy White) has a cleft palate.

Sex Devil attempts to get his fellow classmates to like him. Unfortunately he pretends that he knows karate, which is a lie. Sex Devil's lies are soon discovered. After that his fellow classmates put a thing on the blackboard. It is a picture of Sex Devil (I mean Randy White) with slanting eyes, which he does not have. Underneath the picture it says Wandy Wite, Kawate Kiwwah. Also there is a bubble coming out of Randy White's mouth. Randy White is saying WAH!

A school janitor sees Randy White's humiliation. After school the janitor who is Asian American pulls Randy White to the side. Randy White is apprehensive yet he follows the school janitor to his creepy shack. Underground beneath the shack there is a training facility for a rare form of karate called Jah-Kwo-Ton. Randy White goes there every day and learns how to fight Jah-Kwo-Ton style which nobody else in America knows except the janitor.

The janitor has vowed not to fight because he accidentally killed a man once. He has also made Randy White swear not to defend the janitor in case anything happens to him. The janitor has learned to accept his fate.

One day the same classmates who pick on Randy White accidentally kill the janitor. Well it is partially on purpose and partially on accident. Randy White attempts to aid the janitor but the janitor tells him to remember his vow. Randy White remembers his vow. Now his classmates assume that Randy White is more cowardly than ever.

Now we go forward into the future. Sex Devil can afford the right kind of medical insurance to where his cleft palate can be surgically fixed. While he is pretending to be Randy White he continues to talk like he has a cleft palate. This is just to conceal his secret identity.

All of the boys of Sex Devil's high school class have grown into manhood to become a criminal organization. They run the city under cover of darkness, plotting fake terrorist plots to keep the city in turmoil while they make their robberies. As a result some innocent Arab Americans get sent to prison.

Sex Devil is the prison psychiatrist for the innocent Arab Americans. They can tell that Sex Devil is their friend. The Arab Americans instruct Sex Devil in the ways of a secret cult to where Sex Devil now has ultimate control over his body. Now Sex Devil is an expert in two different secret cults of ancient lore. He is also a trained psychiatrist with mastery over the human mind. No one can match his prowess based on his unique balance of science, skill and sorcery.

Sex Devil finds out from the Arab Americans that the very same people who framed them are the same people who used to pick on Sex Devil all the time. Sex Devil vows revenge.

One night he goes undercover at the chemical factory of his old enemy, who now goes by the name of Black Friday. In the middle of a fight where Black Friday unfairly uses guns Sex Devil gets chemicals spilled on his genital region. Black Friday uses the opportunity to get away.

Sex Devil retreats to his underground lair, which is located beneath the janitor shack. He examines his genital region and discovers that his genital region now has amazing powers. Combined with the bodily control he has learned from the Arab Americans now Sex Devil realizes he has a unique opportunity.

Sex Devil starts out by dating Black Friday's girlfriend. This is the same girl that used to make fun of Sex Devil but she doesn't know it is the same person because he talks completely different.

First Sex Devil takes Jennifer to a nice restaurant. Jennifer is impressed by Sex Devil's worldly manners. Because of his secret mastery of bodily control he is also the best dancer anyone has ever seen. It is the greatest date ever. Jennifer asks Sex Devil if he wants to come up for some coffee. Sex Devil jokes, who knows where that will lead. Sex Devil leaves politely without taking advantage of Jennifer.

When Sex Devil gets home he has about six or seven phone calls from Jennifer on his answering machine. Please Sex Devil, I need to see you.

Sex Devil goes back over to Jennifer's apartment. On the way he stops and buys some flowers. Then he climbs up a drainpipe and enters Jennifer's bedroom.

Jennifer thanks Sex Devil for the flowers. They are so beautiful Sex Devil. Black Friday never buys me flowers. Sex Devil says enough of this talk. Then Sex Devil and Jennifer have intimacy.

Black Friday wonders what is wrong with Jennifer. She seems to be distracted all the time. He does not know she is secretly thinking of her intimacy with Sex Devil. Jennifer refuses to have intimacy with Black Friday. Intimacy with Black Friday has become hollow. Nothing can compare to the amazing powers of Sex Devil's genital region.

Black Friday becomes depressed. Black Friday loses his ability to have intimacy. He must see a psychiatrist. Get me the best psychiatrist in the city! Little does he realize it is Sex Devil.

Black Friday unburdens the problems of his soul to Sex Devil. On the outside Sex Devil is concerned. On the inside Sex Devil is ha ha ha!

Black Friday can no longer do his criminal activities because he has lost all worth of himself as a human being. Black Friday can no longer perform intimacy because of his crippling depression. Every time Black Friday leaves the house Sex Devil comes over and has intimacy with Jennifer. Please Sex Devil I love you, can't we get married? No Jennifer, I am married to my work.

At the end of the first issue Black Friday falls off a cliff. Now Sex Devil must go to work on the rest of the class. At the end of every issue one of Sex Devil's fellow classmates falls off a cliff or is caught in the gears of a large machine or blows themself up in an explosion or capsizes or a similar disaster. Or they are in a submarine that slowly fills up with water. It is never Sex Devil's fault but he doesn't feel bad about it because they are getting what they deserve. Every time Jennifer is like please won't you spend the whole night Sex Devil? What is with all this wham bam thank you mam. And Sex Devil is like maybe some other time baby. Because Sex Devil has more important things on his mind. And Jennifer is like I am starting to think you are just using me for intimacy like a hor. And Sex Devil is like now you are getting the picture baby.

In conclusion I hope you will start making the comic book Sex Devil because it deals with issues that young people care about today.

THE PIPE

The radio station had buried one of its DJs in a field. He was going to stay there for forty-six days to break some kind of a record. There was a clear plastic pipe sticking out of the ground and that was where his air came from. The pipe was as big around as a half-dollar and it came about two feet out of the ground. The station had placed an awning over the pipe so the DJ wouldn't drown if there happened to come a squall. A little electric bell sat on a table with a wire running to it from under the dirt. The DJ was supposed to press a button if he got into trouble, for example, if an animal burrowed its way into his box, or if he started going out of his mind. Then the electric bell would ring and the two men on duty would dig him up right quick.

There were two men on duty all the time. The midnight-to-six shift was taken by a big thick-necked security guard with a shaved head and bright red ears, and a short little paramedic with a pocky face and a black moustache.

"I ain't going to be doing this my entire life," the paramedic said by way of introduction.

"It likely won't come up much," said the security guard. "Somebody alive buried underground on purpose. I don't reckon you'll have to worry about that too often."

"I mean in general," said the paramedic. "I'm talking about servitude. I reckon you think it's pretty great being an EMT."

The security guard did not appear to have an opinion.

"Yes, I guess compared to a security guard you think I got it pretty sweet," the paramedic went on. "A medical professional such as myself is a highly educated man, and as such has very few problems or inner demons. Whereas, anybody can be a security guard."

"Well, not anybody," said the security guard.

"Whoa, now, don't get me wrong! I have the utmost respect for whatever the hell it is that you do. But by nature, I'm just a more complicated man. You're probably... satisfied. Like a cow. I don't mean that in a bad way. But I have yearnings, you get me?"

"I reckon."

"Like creatively, I'd prefer to finish my rock opera I've been working on for some time now. It's set in the high pressure world of paramedics."

"You a rocker?" said the security guard. "I do admire those that can rock."

"I don't fool myself that I can go back to the callow days of youth and all. But nowadays, you can sit on your can at a computer and just come out with rock operas one after another. You can be a composer. That's a respectable job. Rock is an acceptable form of composition in today's world of modernity. I just have to get the right type of computer program and then it's so long to shit details like this! No offense to your way of life."

"I like music. I put myself through junior college working in a record store," said the security guard.

"At least I never sunk that low," said the paramedic.

By one in the morning the last straggling gawkers had long since gone home. The paramedic and the security guard sat on folding chairs and played cards at the little table with the bell on it, their game lit by a hurricane lamp.

"Play again?" said the paramedic.

The security guard shrugged.

The paramedic absently shuffled the deck anyway.

"Reckon what would happen if I dropped some fire ants down that hole," the paramedic said, nodding toward the air pipe.

"I asked you not to talk like that," said the security guard.

"Well, we got a law in this country called freedom of speech. Maybe they didn't teach you about that in security guard school."

"You wouldn't drop nothing down that hole."

"I got a lot of things in back of the ambulance we could try dropping down that hole. Cotton balls, different types of medicine. Needles. If he didn't like it he could ring his little bell and we would stop."

"I can tell you right now he wouldn't like it."

"What if I was to tee-tee down that hole?"

"I wish you'd stop talking that way."

"I'm just using the powers of imagination. Used to be that was okay in this country."

"I wish you'd stop acting smart."

"Just having fun."

"All right then."

"You want to smoke some dope?"

"If you got some."

The paramedic and the security guard smoked a good bit of dope. The paramedic blew some smoke down the hole and they got to laughing about that.

"He didn't ring his bell," said the paramedic.

"He must've liked it," said the security guard.

"Well, that's all he's getting."

They laughed.

"Wonder why somebody would do that," said the security guard, nodding toward the air pipe.

"Publicity," said the paramedic, then he laughed until he cried. The security guard laughed too. The paramedic was laughing at the radio station's gross miscalculation. Why bury your DJ out in the middle of nowhere, where there wasn't any foot traffic or car traffic or any kind of traffic? Why not put a microphone in there with him so he could broadcast his fearsome thoughts as he slowly went mad or what-have-you? Why not put a little TV camera in there with him so people could watch him go crazy? The paramedic stopped laughing and started freaking out.

"We have to dig him up," he said.

"I can't allow that," said the security guard.

"How can he stand it?"

"Maybe he has a troubled home life. Maybe it's an improvement."

"What would you do if I started digging him up? Shoot me?"

"If I had to."

"Wow."

The paramedic decided no more dope tonight.

"God dog I'm hungry," said the security guard.

Day 2

"You want me to stay with you until he gets here?"

"Nah, you been here since suppertime. Go on home," said the security guard.

"What if he never gets here?"

"He'll be here directly."

"What if he ain't?"

"I'm a good digger."

"If it should come to that."

"Right."

"Okay then, I'm going to go home. It's all on your head."

"Yes sir."

"That man's blood is on your hands."

Around two in the morning the security guard's stomach started in to growling real bad. He wished he had some sandwiches.

The security guard squatted on his haunches near the air pipe.

"Hey," he said.

No answer came.

"Hey. What do you eat in there?"

The pipe just made a thin sound like breeze in a conch shell.

The security guard squatted there thinking. He could squat on his haunches all night if he had to. His grandfather had been a farmer. His grandfather had gotten up before daybreak and squatted on his haunches in a field all day long until he was 83 without complaining.

After a little while the security guard said, "I imagine they give you astronaut food."

No answer.

"They probably got a way to mash up a whole entire steak and put it in a tube."

The pipe was silent.

Day 3

"That paramedic of yours ever show up?"

"Nope."

"But you made out okay."

"Pretty fair."

"Maybe he'll show up tonight."

"Could be."

"Don't tell nobody I'm letting you stay out here by yourself."

"Ain't by myself," said the security guard. He patted his gun.

About three-thirty the security guard noticed that he only had half a sandwich left. He was pretty full anyway so he went over to the pipe and squatted down.

"Hey," he said.

"You getting enough to eat in there?

"I got about half a sandwich left, ain't bit into it or anything.

"How about it?

"You want a part of a sandwich?

"It's good, I promise.

"I could roll it up and poke it down this here hole for you.

"Okay, here it comes."

The security guard carefully folded the half-sandwich and pushed it into the pipe.

"Oh, good golly. Don't worry now, but I done clogged up your breathing hole.

"Can you hear me?

"Hold on a second."

He unholstered his gun and tried fishing out the sandwich with the barrel. The sandwich became dislodged and disappeared down the pipe.

Day 4

The security guard was on duty alone again, but this time a number of spectators stayed around well past midnight, probably because it was the weekend.

Finally the security guard stood up and put his hand on his holster.

"Okay folks, show's over," he said.

There was a little bit of a fuss, but they left.

As soon as he was sure the last car had gone, the security guard hurried over to the pipe. He got down on all fours and put his mouth right on it.

"I missed you," he whispered. Then he reverted to his old squatting position.

"I guess that sounds funny," he said after awhile.

After another while he said, "Don't be embarrassed, it sounds funny to me too."

Day 5

"How come you keep staring at that pipe?"

"I ain't staring."

"Ain't you even going to ask me where I been all this time?"

"Okay, where?"

"I got a day job too, you know. Well, an earlier-in-the-night job. When I'm not being a paramedic, saving human lives, I collect quarters out of newspaper vending machines."

"Just quarters?"

"Mostly quarters. Would you stop staring at that damn pipe?"

The security guard closed his eyes and bowed his head and pinched the bridge of his nose.

"Are you going to listen at this or not?"

"Go on and tell it," said the security guard, but he stayed in his clenched-up position.

"Okay, since you ask so nice. The newspaper gives you a company car and you drive all over creation picking up money out of newspaper machines. It's what I like to call a no-brainer. So once in awhile, while I'm driving across the Bay Bridge and it's a pretty nice evening, I like to indulge myself in the occasional reefer. Reward yourself for a job well done, like they say. Well, I've rewarded myself must be a thousand times with no incident. But this *one* night, wouldn't you know I got pulled over by the pigs. That's why I didn't show up. They saw the joint *and* they found a baggie on me *and* I had an open container of whiskey between my knees. Did I happen to mention that?"

The paramedic looked to the security guard for some kind of reaction, which was not forthcoming.

"Anyhow, the pig that's patting me down at the station house, he can feel that I'm wearing a girdle.

"He says, 'You got a back problem, son?'

"And I say, 'Yes, a back problem.'

"So he's patting me down some more and soon enough he gets his hands up under my pants legs. And you *know* what he feels instead of a bare, hairy leg."

The security guard looked up.

"He feels him a pair of nice slippery nylon pantyhose."

"You was wearing *hose*?"

"You heard me."

"Ladies' hose?"

"The very same. You know what the pig said the minute he felt 'em?"

"Did he holler bloody murder?"

"He said, 'Oh.' Just as quiet and flat, no emotion or nothing. Just, 'Oh.' Like that."

The security guard shook his head.

"Why'd you ever come back here?" he said.

"Well, I must say that pig had a better attitude than you. In fact I hate to even call him a pig. What do you reckon he wrote down on the report? 'Wears girdle for back support.' He didn't mention the other. Now he didn't have to do that. He could have wrote a whole lot worse."

"I guess he could've."

"Well, I spent the night in stir and my boss come to bail me out the next day. He had to pick up the company car too, from where they had it impounded. And see, that's how I come to get in another little scrap. When bossman's going through the car, that's when he run across my griftin' sack."

"Your what now?"

"My griftin' sack. See, every machine I emptied for the company, I'd skim, oh, fifty cents or a dollar off the top. Wasn't no way for them to tell. I'd bring back the leftover papers and they could count 'em, I guess, but you know there's always some jackass taking out two or three papers at a time, so the box is always short. It's like they're *asking* you to grab a little for yourself."

"You're disreputable," said the security guard.

"Call it what you will," said the paramedic. He looked satisfied.

Day 6

The paramedic and the security guard had smoked a bunch of dope. The paramedic got up and wobbled toward the pipe.

"Look at me, I'm going to blow some smoke in the hole," he said.

"Oh no you ain't," said the security guard.

The paramedic wheeled around.

"You used to like it when I blowed smoke in the hole."

"I don't like it anymore."

They tried to stare each other down. The security guard won.

The paramedic remained in a funk for the rest of the shift.

Day 7

"You're a lot of fun," the paramedic said.

The security guard stared at the pipe.

"I've got an idea," said the paramedic. "Tomorrow I'm going to bring some M&Ms, and we're going to see who can ring that pipe without getting up."

The security guard jumped up, clutching his chest.

"Oh my God, I just thought of a horrible thing," he said.

"What is it?" said the paramedic.

The security guard sat down heavily.

"Oh my God," he said.

He put his hands over his face.

"What's the matter?"

"I put part of a sandwich in that pipe the other night. I was trying to unstick it and it fell down into the hole."

"So what? It was all in good fun I'm sure."

"I mean, what if that sandwich didn't go all the way down the pipe? There's got to be at least four more foot of pipe below ground. What if it got jammed somewhere we can't see it? What if it clogged off the air?"

"Is that all? Listen. If something was to cut off the air supply, don't you know that hombre would be buzzing his little bell for all it was worth? Naw, I wouldn't worry about it."

"What if there's a problem with the bell, like a short circuit? What if he mashed the button and nothing happened? What if he was asleep when the sandwich come down and he didn't know he was losing air? Or what if the oxygen stopped flowing and it just made him peaceful and dizzy-like and he just kind of drifted off and died in a slumber?"

"Now I'm sure the people that designed this here bell had all that in mind. Don't you think they considered every possibility? I think they know a tee-nincey bit more about oxygen and bells and all than you and me do. I wouldn't be surprised if this here bell was hooked up in such a way as to monitor his vital signs, and the split second his pulse started in to slowing down or his breathing became erratic or what-have-you, that little bell would just ring off the hook without him having to lay a finger on it. It's called the process of science."

"What if the bell rang and I didn't hear it because I was blacked out?"

"Do you black out a lot?"

"Not to my knowledge, but I wouldn't know it if I did, now would I?"

"Sure you would. You'd wake up in a ditch or somewheres. Or, you know, 'How'd this blood get on my shirt?' Stuff like that. You're just having 'what if' thoughts. That's a classic sign of clinical anxiety, that's all that is."

The security guard sat up straight and looked at the pipe.

"So you think he's okay?"

"Oh, hell yeah. He's like a piece of property to that radio station. You think they're going to let something happen to him? How would that look? They probably check on him all the time."

"How?"

"I don't know. He probably has a phone in there with him. They probably got it fixed up nicer than my house. I'd trade places with him in a heartbeat. People pay a lot of money at these health spas to climb in a tank like that and close the lid. It's soothing."

"You was all for digging him up the other night."

"I was all for a lot of things the other night. I was as high as Sputnik."

"I would've known if something bad had happened, right? Something would've told me. I would've felt something in my bones."

"Oh, hell yeah, bro. Are you kidding me? You would've felt the cold hand of death. I feel it all the time."

The security guard looked at the pipe.

"Oh, he's fine," he said. "You can tell."

"Hey, do you want some pills?"

"What kind of pills?"

"Make-you-feel-better pills."

"Just a few I guess."

Day 8

"Did I ever tell you about the boil I developed?"

"Not to my recollection."

"Oh, you'd remember it if I told you. Reckon you can guess where it was located."

"Your behind?"

"Bingo. All the other paramedics said it was the biggest one they'd ever seen."

"Must've been pretty big."

"Let me put it to you this way. I had to check myself into the hospital to get that sucker drained. They come out with two whole measuring cups full of stuff."

"What kind of stuff?"

"Awful stuff."

Day 9

The paramedic returned from taking a whiz.

"What's going on here?"

The security guard scrambled to his feet.

"Nothing."

"What were you doing to the pipe?"

"Checking it for dirt and other obstructive materials."

"Looked like you were having a conversation with it."

"What kind of conversation?"

"A friendly conversation."

"I don't know what you're talking about. I was checking it for dirt."

"Hey, as long as you're not humping it, that's all I care about."

Day 10

The paramedic's girlfriend showed up with a six-pack. The security guard rose so she could have a seat. She was a lively, dwarfish young woman with yellow hair, a red checked shirt and denim shorts.

"Aren't you polite?" she said.

She declined his offer and sat instead on the paramedic's lap. They acted silly. The paramedic's girlfriend looked at the security guard and whispered something in the paramedic's ear. They busted out laughing.

"She thinks—" said the paramedic, but his girlfriend pinched him so hard he yelped and couldn't finish his sentence.

"This is boring," said the girlfriend.

"It was until you come along," said the paramedic. He goosed her and she squealed.

The girlfriend finished her beer and surveyed the awning, and the pipe, and the empty field. "I don't get the big attraction," she said.

"You're looking at it," said the paramedic.

"I bet there's nobody on the other end of that pipe at all."

"Yes there is," said the security guard.

"How do you know?"

"It would be false advertising if there wasn't. They'd get hauled up before a judge and get their FCC license snatched away from them. Anyway, there's been somebody here one hundred percent of the time since they planted him in the ground. Somebody would've seen him if he'd crawled out."

"They probably got a tunnel under there that runs clear to town. He's probably holed up at a whorehouse laying low and he'll crawl back into that box just before they dig him up."

"Now what would you know about whorehouses?" said the paramedic.

She slapped him.

"You're bad," she said.

"Your plan is illogical," said the security guard. "A tunnel of that length would be prohibitive."

"Well now, let's not be too hasty," said the paramedic.

"That's right, you take up for me," said the girlfriend.

"If you'd hush up for two seconds, that's what I'm trying to do. Say it ain't a tunnel. Granted. But you got to admit there's plenty of ways of fooling the eye in the world of magic and illusion. When the fellow saws the lady in half, everybody's watching like you say. But that don't mean he really saws her in half."

"How do they do that?" said the girlfriend.

"Two ladies," said the paramedic.

The security guard got up and rubbed his hands together.

"I think you're missing the point," he said. "It's not a trick. It's a feat of human endurance. They're trying to break a record. If it's a trick, they just defeat their whole purpose. If it's a trick, why are we out here guarding it every night?"

"Maybe we're part of the *illusion*," the paramedic said in a dramatic voice. He waved his hands in swirling patterns like a magician, and his girlfriend giggled.

"I don't think it's funny," said the security guard. He stomped off far away from them, kicking up clods of dirt. Later he shot two bullets into a tree.

Day 11

The lanky redhead went to powder her nose.

"Are you planning on bringing a different girl out here every night?"

"She ain't exactly a girl."

"What is she, a lady?"

"Let's put it this way. She has the same thing in her pants as you and me."

The security guard was startled.

"What's the matter, cat got your tongue?"

"No."

"Do I shock you with my unconventional ways?"

"Look. I don't care what she's got in her pants. All I'm saying is, she's not allowed around here."

"Are you prejudiced against her because she's different?"

"No."

"Because that's called sexual harassment and it's against the law."

"I just don't want you to create a hazardous and distracting work environment. We're not supposed to have guests. I should have mentioned it last night when you brung your other girlfriend."

"Where is that written? In the book of you?"

The redhead came back and the conversation snapped shut.

"Gracious," she said. "My ears are burning."

"We're just talking about work stuff, baby. You wouldn't be interested."

"Y'all should get a radio out here."

She started singing a song about everybody shaking their bodies and doing the conga. She danced in a snaky and graceful manner as she sang.

"I'm going to have to ask you to cease and desist," said the security guard.

"What are you going to do, shoot her?" said the paramedic.

"What's the matter, sweetie?" she said to the security guard. "Can I try on your hat?"

"No."

The redhead crossed her arms and pretended to pout.

"I'm sorry to interfere with your singing and dancing," said the security guard. "It's very nice and pleasant, but now is neither the time nor the place."

"Watch out or he'll shoot you," said the paramedic.

"He would not. Just look at those eyes. He's a big, fierce overgrown lamb is what he is."

"Is that what you think? Last night he shot a tree. He considers it his personal duty to shoot anything that's beautiful in this world."

The security guard sighed.

"Don't let him get to you, sugar. He likes to tease is all."

"I know that," said the security guard. "What I'm trying to explain, ma'am, is that if you sing that way, we're liable not to hear this bell if it rings."

"Teacher says every time a bell rings an angel gets its wings."

"That's precisely what we don't want happening in this case, ma'am," said the security guard.

Day 12

The redhead came back. The security guard didn't mind. She was respectful and kept her promise not to be too rowdy or get in the way. Everyone had sandwiches and then the paramedic nodded at the redhead in a manner that suggested *Come with me.*

"I promised I'd show her something in the ambulance," he told the security guard.

They climbed the fence and crossed the ditch and got into the back of the ambulance, leaving the security guard alone. He waited awhile to make sure they weren't coming back and then he went over and sat next to the pipe.

"Hey," he said.

"Sorry I haven't been more attentive."

He sat there a few seconds.

"You know how it is," he said.

He looked at the ambulance, which seemed still and innocent.

"I hope you're doing okay.

"You know you can tell me if you need anything.

"Just give a signal."

This time he was smart. He got up and brushed the dry grass off his knees and returned to his chair so he wouldn't have to hear any of the paramedic's wisecracks. He picked up the pack of cards and looked through them, like maybe he'd find one nobody had ever seen before. Pretty soon the paramedic came back, smoking a cigarette.

"Where's your friend?"

"Resting up. Cigareet?"

"No thanks. Got any dope?"

"Not tonight. Not on me. You know, it wouldn't hurt you to chip in on the dope, by the way."

"Oh! Okay."

"I mean, it's not like I have dope growing out of my ass. I mean, I have many talents, but dope growing out of my ass is not among them."

"I've been neglectful."

"No hard feelings. I just wanted to bring that issue out in the open. Anything exciting happen while I was gone?"

"No."

"The moon didn't come crashing down into the earth?"

"Not that I'm aware of."

"Well, that's good. What you been doing? Communing with your pipe?"

"Now why would you say something ugly like that?"

"Easy, cowboy. Just busting your chops. Remember when I saw you talking to the pipe that time?"

"I have never in my life talked to that pipe."

Day 13

The paramedic and the redhead were in the back of the ambulance. The security guard didn't go near the pipe.

Day 14

"Are you in love with her?"

"What's love?"

"You have a bad attitude."

"I get by with it."

The security guard shook his head.

"She's real nice," he said.

"She's okay," said the paramedic. "She's a he."

"I've decided not to believe you on that score."

"Believe what you will, my friend. Believe what you will. You ever notice how they do that in the movies? They say something, then they say 'friend,' then they repeat the first thing they said. That's a stupid way to talk."

"Don't you think she ever gets tired of just being fidgeted with in the back of an ambulance every night of the week?"

They gazed across the barbed wire and the muddy trench where the crawdads were chirruping toward the dark and silent ambulance, inside which the redhead was resting up.

"Don't seem very romantic anyway."

"Never said it was, friend. Never said it was."

Day 15

The security guard had talked the paramedic into taking a few days off and treating his redheaded friend right. He had given the paramedic fifty dollars for a night on the town and promised to sign his timecard for him until he decided to come back.

"It's just you and me tonight," he said to the pipe.

Day 16

The security guard talked about a frog he had accidentally mashed in a screen door and a bird he had hit with his car and a dog of his youth that had been run over by a bread truck before his eyes. He cried a good bit. It felt good to cry.

Day 17

"I don't know if it was Down's Syndrome or not. There was a whole busload of them. These two came in and I remember they wanted to buy a cassette single of David Lee Roth singing 'Yankee Rose.' You're a DJ, you probably remember that. I think he was done up in face paint on the cover, like a native or something. Anyway, they put their money on the counter and it was nothing but a bunch of pennies. It was way under two hundred pennies, or however many pennies it was going to take, but they kept insisting that I count the pennies, and I didn't want to hurt their feelings or anything, so. And they would get in there and mess me up while I was trying to count, because they were, you know. Once in awhile one of them would find another penny and throw it into the stack I was trying to count. So finally I just said, 'Hey, I'm sure this will be fine. Why don't you go ahead and take this cassette and I'll count these pennies later? I'll pay for whatever's left over.' So they took their David Lee Roth and headed out, and when they got to the door one of them stopped and said to me, real mean, 'I guess you think you're a great person now.' And she kind of stormed out. I always heard that Down's Syndrome people were real sweet and tried to hug you, but this one was mean. She really hurt my feelings."

Day 18

"He says, 'I used to ride the school bus with you,' and I say, 'Oh, right, right!'

"He says, 'You know, Fat Boy That Lives in the Log Cabin House.'

"I'm, you know, 'Huh?'

"And he turns to his friend and says, 'That's what they used to call me. Fat Boy That Lives in the Log Cabin House.'

"And I say, uh, 'I don't believe *I* called you that.'

"He says, 'Oh yes you did.' And then he made fun of me for being a security guard, like 'Nice uniform,' and so on."

Day 19

"It was supposed to be a costume party but I was the only one that dressed up. I was a tin soldier, I had rouge on my cheeks and everything. I had an allergic reaction to it. My eyes were burning and they couldn't get it to come off. They scrubbed my face raw and it still wouldn't come off.

Then Bill Clements told everybody at school that my mother kept a dirty house. I forget how it came up, but he said it right in front of the teacher and everybody. He raised his hand before he said it, like it was a math question. That was first grade. In ninth grade Jed Humphries broke my nose on purpose, but he pretended it was an accident so he didn't get into trouble. He'd pretend to be your friend so you'd tell him whatever secret it was, and then he'd use it to make fun of you like a month or two later after you forgot all about it. I sure hope he turned out worse off than me."

Day 20

"Are you mad at me?

"I'm just asking because sometimes it seems like you're ignoring me.

"I know I'm just being sensitive.

"Anyway, here I am, gripe, gripe, gripe, and we never talk about what's going on with *you*.

"And I really want to apologize for that.

"These past few days have meant a lot to me, and I guess I'd just appreciate it..."

The security guard's throat felt hard, like his Adam's apple was a chunk of marble. He made a snorting noise unfamiliar to himself and a tear came loose from his eye and fell silently into the pipe.

"I guess I'd just appreciate it if I got some sort of acknowledgement that you felt the same way.

"Or just, you know, tell me to shut up and go away!"

Day 21

"Where's your friend?"

"She won't be joining us."

"How come?"

"We split."

"Sorry."

"Eh."

"She was nice."

"I reckon."

"What happened to the other one?"

"The midget?"

"Yeah."

"I'm not real sure."

"She wasn't a midget, was she?"

"Close enough."

"Huh."

"Anything exciting happen while I was gone?"

"No."

"Hey, I want to thank you for fudging my timesheet."

"No problem."

"I mean, you didn't have to do that."

"You're a good guy. A little on the rowdy side. But unlike some people at least you know how to carry on a polite conversation."

"Why are you yelling all of a sudden?"

"Was I yelling?"

Day 22

Dope.

"If I tell you something will you promise not to think I'm crazy?"

"I'll try."

The security guard started crying.

"Easy there, cowboy," said the paramedic.

The security guard dried his eyes.

"I have been talking to that pipe, just like you said."

"No shit," said the paramedic, seeming to marvel a little.

"Yeah. Many's the time I've set by that pipe and just talked away."

"Wow. What about?"

"I, you know, I try to keep him company, keep his spirits up or whatever."

"Do you read him the funny pages?"

"Not exactly."

"Well, what then?"

"I don't know. Just talk."

"Chit chat?"

The security guard shrugged.

"*No shit*," said the paramedic. His eyes were large and bright. He sprang up from his chair.

The security guard jumped up after him.

"Where are you going?" he said.

"Hell, I'm going to talk to the pipe," said the paramedic.

"Wait," said the security guard, but it was too late.

"Hey pipe," said the paramedic. "How's it going?"

"No, no," said the security guard. He came over and sat on the ground. The paramedic sat beside him.

"Now you say something," said the paramedic.

"That's not the way..." The security guard put his head in his hands.

"What, am I doing it wrong?" The paramedic leaned over, cupped his hands around his mouth and put his mouth right over the pipe. "Sorry!" he shouted.

He sat up again.

"Now what do we do?" said the paramedic. "This is awesome."

"Who cares?" the security guard said, muffled through his hands. "It doesn't matter."

"What's eating you?"

The security guard looked up and shook his head.

"Wait a minute. Did you hear that just now?" said the paramedic.

The security guard became alert.

"There it was again," said the paramedic.

He put his ear down to the opening and listened.

"Uh-huh, uh-huh," said the paramedic.

"What? *What*?" said the security guard.

The paramedic sat up.

"He said he sure wished you'd stop putting your weenie in the hole."

Day 23

"I can't *believe* that fucker won't talk to us."

"I'm sorry I brought it up. It's just silliness. It's not his job to talk to us. It's *our* job to guard him. Nothing personal. I was pretty hurt and upset at first, but now I've prayed about it and I've really come to make peace with it in my own heart. Who cares if he talks to us or not? We're not getting paid to talk to him and he's not getting paid to talk to us. It's plain economics."

"You put your finger on it, bro. You're out here every night guarding his ass from vandals and coyotes and what-have-you, and I'm here standing by with the snakebite kit and the defibrillator paddles, midnight-to-six like clockwork, and what's he doing? Lying in a hole? And that makes him too good to talk to us? Hell, we ought to be his favorite people in the world. He ought to be talking our damn ears off. Watch this."

The paramedic got up and strode over to the pipe. The security guard followed.

"You're not going to do anything drastic are you?" said the security guard.

The paramedic put a finger to his lips. Both men squatted near the pipe.

"Hey, how's the weather down there?" said the paramedic.

They listened. Nothing.

"Hey, I'm talking to you, pipe boy," said the paramedic. "That's okay, that's okay. You just keep your own counsel. Meanwhile, I'm going to open up this box my cousin give me."

The paramedic pantomimed flipping the latches on a box.

"Hand me those forceps, will you?" he said to the security guard.

The security guard stared at him.

The paramedic held out his hand emphatically, as if he really expected some forceps to be slapped into them. The security guard shrugged and pretended as best he could to hand the paramedic some forceps.

"Thanks, bro," said the paramedic. Then, to the hole: "My cousin Jojo works in a pet shop and he loaned me a whole bunch of baby scorpions. I promised to return 'em, but I seriously doubt they'll miss five or six of these little devils. I got a whole mess of 'em here. Hold on now, I'm going to catch one in these forceps. All right, I got one, and now I'm holding it right over your air hole. Easy, little fella! Don't get too impatient now! He looks hungry to me. He's just wriggling like a little puppy hankering for mother's milk. You wouldn't mind getting a visit from a hungry baby scorpion, would you? It's up to you. All you have to do is say the word, and I'll put him right back in the box. Just say, 'No thanks!' Just say, 'No scorpions for me tonight, thanks!' Just say, 'I'll pass!'"

They listened.

"You better say something, or I swear to God there's a deadly scorpion heading straight down this hole!"

Nothing.

"Here it comes!"

They sat there for a few seconds, the paramedic holding the invisible forceps over the pipe.

"You win this round," he said at last.

He pretended to put the scorpion back in its box.

Day 24

They made a pact to ignore the pipe. They played cards and ate sandwiches and drank beer, but their hearts weren't in it. When the paramedic went off to take a whiz, the security guard walked over and addressed the pipe.

"Sorry about last night," he said. "He was just trying to rile you. Please don't get him in hot water when they dig you up. He was just trying to get a rise out of you, no harm done. He didn't have no scorpions. He's a nice type person. I hope we can put this all behind us."

"Hey! What do you think you're doing?"

The security guard turned and saw the paramedic galloping toward him, zipping his pants.

"We made a vow!"

"I know."

Now the short little paramedic had arrived and he stood toe-to-toe with the security guard, panting, looking up, his frog eyes popping out of his head.

"What's the big idea then?"

"I was just setting the record straight."

"About what?"

"About you."

"I can take up for myself, thank you very much."

"Okay."

"I know whose side you're on."

"I'm not on anybody's side."

"Right. If somebody popped out of the bushes to rape me right this minute, and somebody else was about to kick over that pipe at the exact same time, don't you think I know which one of us you'd protect?"

The security guard didn't say anything.

"That's what I thought!" said the paramedic.

He hurried to the ambulance, got in and drove away with the siren going full blast.

Day 25

It was raining when the security guard arrived for duty. He didn't expect the paramedic to show, and he was right.

By two in the morning the rain had turned into something Biblical. The table fell over. The awning blew away in the gale. The security guard had to remove his poncho and use it to keep the pipe from filling up with water. He became soaked to the bone. He shivered and shook as he kept the water away from the pipe and made sure at the same time that the poncho did not cut off the air. It was a delicate balancing act that required all his concentration and exhausted him, mentally and physically. The wind howled and the rain came down.

Day 26

Alone again.

Burning up with fever.

Racked with chills.

The security guard's head throbbed so bad that it looked like the stars were twitching and dancing over the field. He started seeing people walking by, some of whom he recognized as dead. He tried making conversation with them through his cracked lips.

An imp rose up from the field, a little black thing with a pointed head and orange eyes, looked to be about two feet tall.

"Oh no you don't, you stay away from that pipe," said the security guard, or seemed to say it.

The imp grinned at him.

Imp poked at pipe with crooked black claw-ended stick.

Silver dust started puffing up out of the pipe, like when you step on a toadstool.

The security guard got up and started toward the pipe.

He collapsed.

Day 27

"Okay, here I am," said the paramedic. "What's the big emergency? Somebody die?"

"Not yet," said the supervisor.

"What do you mean, not yet?"

"The man you were supposed to be working with last night, that's what I'm talking about. The man who was laying there on the ground in need of some medical attention, which you were supposed to be here to give. Where were you?"

"What happened?"

"Are you going to answer my question?"

"My dog was sick."

"I've heard a lot of unpleasant things about you, junior."

"From who?"

"Just in general. You're a fairly well-known shitheel."

"Thank you."

"Maybe you'll wipe that little shit-sniffing smirk off your pig-faced kisser when I introduce you to your new partner."

"And who would that be?"

"Me," said the supervisor.

Day 28

The supervisor made fun of everything the paramedic said or did. He also mocked his face and his stature—even though the supervisor and the paramedic were practically twins.

Ordinarily the paramedic wouldn't have come back for a second night of it, but he needed the money and unlike the security guard, the supervisor could have fired him.

"You sure are homely," said the supervisor. "I despise the thought of sitting here and looking at you all night. Did I just see your lips move, boy?"

"I don't think so," said the paramedic.

"You don't *think* so. Who told you you could think? Your mama?"

Day 29

The weather had cooled off some since the big storm. The paramedic crushed up all kinds of pills and put them into a thermos of hot chocolate.

"Want some hot chocolate?"

"Did your mama make it for you?"

"Yes sir. As a matter of fact she did," the paramedic said humbly.

"Well, ooh-la-la. Ain't that sweet. Mommy's little man."

The paramedic poured some of the steaming chocolate into a styrofoam cup. He bowed his head over it and inhaled the steam.

"Mm-*mm*," he said.

"What'd she do, pee in it? Is that why you think it smells so good?"

The paramedic raised the cup and pretended to drink some of it.

"Boy howdy," he said.

"Really hits the spot, huh," said the supervisor. "A big old cup of mama's pee."

The paramedic emptied the cup on the ground with a harsh, jerky motion.

"What's the matter, Pee Man? Not enough pee in it for you?"

"Well, I can't enjoy it now," said the paramedic.

"Boo hoo hoo. I'm going to give you some free advice, junior. This is a tough world. There's a lot of people in it even tougher than me, believe it or not. You think if you was in the army your drill sergeant wouldn't be ten times as mean as I am? What are you going to do, cry and throw your chocolate on the ground every time somebody says something you don't like? If I lived my life the way you do I couldn't even look at my own face in the mirror. I'd cut my throat from ear to ear rather than live in cowardice like a slimy rat."

He went on like that for a period of time.

The paramedic screwed the lid back on the thermos.

Day 30

The paramedic prepared two thermoses of chocolate. One was normal and the other was spiked with a large variety of powdered medications and some of the paramedic's urine. He put a piece of masking tape on that one to mark it.

At one point the supervisor mentioned how goddamned cold it was getting.

"That reminds me," said the paramedic.

He brought out the two thermoses.

"Well, well, well. La-di-freaking-da," said the supervisor.

"It's hot chocolate," said the paramedic. "One for me and one for you. When I told mama I had a partner out here, she insisted."

"Yeah, I know, she already told me last night while I was putting the stones to her."

The supervisor imitated the sounds of the paramedic's mother having an orgasm.

The paramedic pretended to be sad. He poured himself some hot chocolate from the untainted thermos and began to drink it. The supervisor watched him.

"Shit, if you're going to be pouty about it."

The supervisor removed his thermos's red lid, which doubled as a cup. He unscrewed the inner cap and poured himself some hot chocolate. He brought it up to his nose.

"Now that's some good-smelling chocolate," he said. "Smells just like your mama's coochie."

Pretty soon he had drunk half the thermos.

Not long after that he was holding onto the seat of his chair like he thought it was going to fly out from under him.

"Here we go!" he said.

"Where we going?" said the paramedic.

"Ooooooohhh!" said the supervisor. He ducked.

"Are they after you?" said the paramedic.

The supervisor had some spit coming out of his mouth. He slouched over until his head was between his knees. He moaned for a couple of minutes then he kind of rolled out of his chair in a clumsy, slow somersault and landed on his back.

The paramedic went over and felt his neck, to see if it was broken. It wasn't. He got his stethoscope and listened to the supervisor's heart. It was thumping way too hard and fast, like a dog's leg scratching fleas.

The paramedic returned to his chair and took a pint of whiskey from his black bag. He began dosing his chocolate with it. It tasted good. He practiced some card tricks. Once in awhile he'd look over and make sure the supervisor's chest was still jerking with the breath of life.

Round about dawn the supervisor rose to his hands and knees and vomited a great quantity of stuff.

"What's wrong with me?" he said.

The paramedic lazed over and helped him into his chair.

"You need to take it easy, chief. You have all the symptoms of the Spanish influenza. Why I've had my eye on you all night."

The paramedic told him to stay under a load of blankets and drink lots of 7-Up and take it easy for the rest of the day. He also gave him some devastating laxatives, which he described as vitamin C.

Day 31

The supervisor did not show up.

Having longed for and engineered his own solitude, the paramedic found that he did not particularly enjoy it.

It gave him time to think.

He looked around and thought, So this is it.

This is what it all boils down to.

This is what you're fit for in the eyes of society.

When people ask you what you do, this is what you have to tell them.

I sit in a field all night watching a pipe and waiting for a bell to ring.

And if the bell rings I dig a guy up and keep him from choking on a piece of candy.

He asked himself didn't kings and baseball players and TV stars feel the same way at times, and he told himself probably not.

Probably that's just reserved for jack-offs like you.

He had been absently watching the pipe for a while, reflected light making it seem whitish against the brownish dark, not actively seeing it, his eyes merely resting there, and suddenly he realized that his eyes had crossed and the pipe had become a shivering, blurred pillar of light. He shook his head to clear it.

Soon, though, he allowed himself to drift.

The paramedic entertained a waking dream of the time he had been in a band.

He had been so tender and green!

Pleasant memories overcame him.

I should go get my guitar, he thought. I'll need to restring it. All the time I'm sitting here doing nothing I could be working up some new songs. They'll be better than my old songs, because now I've had more experiences. I've seen and done some crazy shit. That'll come through in the music, and people will respond to it with their guts. *This guy has been around the block.*

The paramedic abandoned his post and left the pipe unattended. He drove into the city to get his guitar and returned with it an hour and a half later. When he stepped out of the ambulance he saw that a large, lean, wolfish dog had made a good amount of headway digging up the spot where the DJ was buried.

The paramedic reached in and hit a button, causing the loudspeakers on top of the ambulance to give a sharp, rude airhorn blast. The dog took off.

Day 32

Headlights. Tires crunching to a stop on the shell road.

The paramedic wiped his mouth, put the cap on the bottle of Goldschlager he had been drinking and stood up.

Here came a tall young brown-skinned stranger, broom-thin, in a dark rumpled hat and a long tan coat.

When the stranger got as far as the ditch that separated the road from the field, the paramedic yelled out, "Halt!"

The stranger laughed, as if he could tell that the paramedic had never used that word before.

"Spectators are required to stay on that side of the ditch," said the paramedic.

The stranger laughed again.

"Spectator?" he said. "What's there to spectate?"

"Well, you have a point," said the paramedic.

"Anyway, I'm not a spectator." The stranger flashed a badge.

A few minutes later he was sitting in the chair opposite the paramedic.

"No," he said, "I'm aware of the current charges filed against you, of course, but as long as you show up for your court appearances, I have no beef with you on that account."

"You got a heart as big as all outdoors," said the paramedic. "Any more at home like you?"

"Or I know what. How about I ask the questions," said the detective.

"Yeah, I've seen that movie. 'I'm the one asking the questions, dirtbag.'"

The detective laughed.

"You sure are one happy cop."

"I love my work."

The paramedic eyed the Goldschlager.

"Go ahead," said the detective. "I want you to be happy too."

"Right. And then you bust me for an open container."

"Trust me, I have bigger fish to fry."

The paramedic studied the detective for a minute. The detective wore an open, friendly set of crooked teeth.

Finally the paramedic had a drink, then he tilted the bottle toward the detective, who shook his head.

"Not when I'm on duty, ma'am," said the paramedic. "I've seen that movie too."

"My second time out here today," said the detective. "I was out here this morning."

"Is that right?"

"Yep. The early shift was kind of, uh, *disappointed* because the area around that pipe over there was pretty much of a wreck, and the responsibility fell on them to clean up the mess. A mess that somebody else had made. They would have asked you about it, but nobody was here when they showed up. According to the roster, you were supposed to be here till six."

"Is that what this is about? I put a monkey wrench in their little freak show? What is that, dereliction of duty, destruction of private property? No, wait, forcing a crew of lazy fat asses to fill up a hole against their will."

"Where were you this morning when you were supposed to be finishing your shift?"

“I left early.”

“Why?”

“Well, I was writing a song on my guitar here, and it was going good, real good, and I wanted to get home and write down the words before I forgot ‘em. And I didn’t have a pen on me.”

“You want to play me a little of this so-called song?”

“Why should I?”

“Well, it might convince me that your story holds some water.”

“Are you trying to make fun of me? Is that some kind of technique they teach you to crush people’s spirits?”

“Oh, now. Let’s just say I’m a music lover.”

The paramedic rubbed his chin for a second, then he picked up the guitar and began to sing:

Half-hearted when you told me that you loved me

Half-hearted when you said that you could care

The detective laughed. He laughed so hard that he began to weep.

The paramedic didn’t say anything.

The detective said, “What’s the name of that song?”

“Half-hearted,” said the paramedic, cold and quiet.

The detective laughed again. He almost choked.

“Oh!” he said. “Oh! Oh! I thought…”

He laughed some more, frail from it.

“I thought you said… I… I *farted* when you told me that you loved me!”

He had another fit.

“Good Lord. That’s the best laugh I’ve had in a coon’s age. I believe I will have a drink.”

He took one, and coughed.

“What’s that stuff floating around in there?”

“Twenty-four carat gold flakes. That’s how it comes.”

“Nasty. Feels like swallowing a bug. Still, it must be pretty expensive, drinking solid gold liquor. You come into some extra money lately?”

“My grandmother give me five dollars for my birthday. You can shake her down if you want to.”

The detective looked at the guitar in the paramedic’s hands.

"You got a second verse you want to do for me? She held my hand and all of a sudden I couldn't help but fart?" He laughed.

The paramedic put down the guitar. The detective watched him.

"Okay. Say you left early to get that little gem committed to paper. Assuming that's the case, how do you explain the hole you left behind?"

"A dog dug it."

"What kind of dog?"

"Looked like a wolf."

"Are you trying to tell me a wolf dug the hole? What is this, some kind of fairy story?"

"No."

"Are we in fairyland?"

"Don't look like it."

"Do you see Tinkerbell anywhere around here?"

The paramedic glared.

"No Tinkerbell. I'll make a note of that. But you still haven't answered my question. Was it a dog or a wolf you supposedly saw?"

"A dog."

"Okay then. Now you're starting to make a little sense. Dogs are part of the real world we all live in. We can all agree on that. I'm glad we're on the same page. Something bothers me, though. Must have been a mighty busy dog. Made a real shambles of the place."

"Well, you know, I was going to fix it up but then I thought what the hell. I mean, I had a song I wanted to work on, whether you like it or not. 'Half-hearted' does not sound like 'I farted,' by the way, unless you're deaf."

"Don't get me to laughing," said the detective.

"Anyway I was by myself. Why should I have to do all that work by myself? It's supposed to be a two-man crew. Nothing in my job description about filling up a hole. I'm only supposed to be here in case of emergency anyway."

"I don't know. A ferocious wolf clawing his way toward an innocent man trapped in a box, that sounds like an emergency in my book. And you're trying to tell me that all the time this rabid animal was clearing out this enormous excavation with his giant paws the size of shovels you just sat here and did nothing?"

"I scared him off."

"And how'd you do that?"

The paramedic gestured toward the ambulance.

"Give the siren a blast."

"But first you gave the Big Bad Wolf plenty of leeway, plenty of, uh, *elbow room* to dig himself a great big hole."

"I wasn't here, man! Okay? I went home to get my guitar."

"And this was *prior* to your going home to get the pen? Two separate trips?"

"Yes."

The detective made a note on his little pad for the first time. He looked up.

"Are you sure you didn't dig that hole?" he said.

"Why would I dig a hole?"

"Maybe you had to bury something. Or maybe you had to dig something up."

"What are you talking about?"

"When was the last time you saw your supervisor?" the detective said.

Day 33

"It's been like a fricking nuthouse around here. I thought they were going to slap the cuffs on me, bro."

"I know. They came to the hospital and asked me a few questions," said the security guard.

"You're shitting me," said the paramedic.

"I am not," said the security guard.

"What did you tell them?"

"I answered all their questions in a complete and truthful way."

"Oh, shit. What does that mean?"

"Shouldn't mean anything to an innocent man."

Day 34

Half-hearted when you told me that you loved me

Half-hearted when you said that you could care

The paramedic stopped strumming.

"Hey, in your opinion was I just singing about farting?"

"Yes," said the security guard.

"Why didn't you laugh?"

"It wasn't funny."

Day 35

"I tell you what I can't stand. Waiting for the other shoe to drop. If they're going to arrest me, why don't they just arrest me? I didn't do anything. Why am I so worried if I didn't do anything? Why does my brain do me that way? What is it with guilt?"

"I don't know," said the security guard.

"Well, I did do one thing. I drugged that fucker so he would get off my back. He just kept riding me, I couldn't take it anymore. This is just between me and you, okay?"

"If they ask me any questions I have to tell them the truth."

"Oh, shit! All I did was give him a few pills so's he'd take a little nap and leave me alone. Are you a narc? Are you here to narc on me? You look like shit, bro. You've turned kind of yellow-looking, did you know that? You're as yellow as the autumn fucking leaves. And you must've lost about twenty pounds. The skin's just sagging off your yellow face. I been wondering and wondering how they ever let you out looking the way you do. Did they let you out early so you could come here and weasel something out of me? That's pretty low, brother. Are you wearing a wire?"

"They told me I should keep resting for another week, but I just can't stand being cooped up. I wanted to get back to work. Ain't nothing wrong with that."

"Yeah, the Judeo-Christian work ethic. Where's the microphone? Is it in your lapel?"

The paramedic stood up, came over, bent down and yelled into the security guard's chest.

"Because I sure do think it's interesting, reminiscing about all those good times we had together! All those times you and me did illegal things like smoking pot and popping pills and drinking booze on the job!"

He straightened up.

"Jesus, the breath coming out of you!" he said.

"Can't help it, I'm sick," said the security guard.

Day 36

"Can you believe that pig came over and harassed me in my own apartment, where I live with my elderly grandmother? He started picking up my snow globes and shaking 'em real hard. I told him, 'Hey, those are for display only,' and he laughed at me. What's so funny? They're in a certain order. People collect all kinds of things, there's nothing funny about it.

"I tell you I was climbing the *walls* when he left. I sprayed every snow globe with Lysol. I even picked 'em up and sprayed underneath. Felt like they had pig smell all over 'em. I had to take half the medicine chest before I could get to sleep. And then I had to take the other half to get up and come out here tonight.

"But the good thing is, I had a *vision*, bro. Or a dream or what-have-you. Anyway, when I woke up I had an airtight alibi! I don't know why I didn't think of it before."

The security guard was silent. The paramedic was silent. The paramedic stared at the security guard. The security guard stared at the moths flitting over the orange moon.

"Don't you want to hear it?" said the paramedic.

The security guard was silent. Or perhaps he was humming very, very faintly.

"Don't you want to hear my alibi?"

The security guard drew a deep breath and let it out in a yawn.

"Okay," he said.

The paramedic jumped up.

"It's a good one! See, what we've been forgetting is there's a *witness* to my last encounter with the alleged victim. A *silent* witness, your honor."

The paramedic picked up a shovel and started toward the pipe. The security guard stood up, wobbly. He had to steady himself with one hand on the table.

"Hold it right there," he said.

The paramedic turned around.

"What do you think you're doing?" said the security guard.

"I'm going to dig that sucker up and put him on the stand."

"I can't allow that," said the security guard. He lurched forward.

"Man, you shouldn't even be on your feet yet."

"I'm fine."

"Well, I'm not. I don't know if I've made it clear enough for you, but the man wants me to burn in the chair, bro. All they got to do is find the body and do the DNA on it or whatever they call it. They'll trace them pills right back to me and that's all she wrote."

The security guard put his hand on his holster.

"Easy, cowboy. I'm putting the shovel down, see? Hey, I've got an idea. We won't dig him up, but how about if we sit over here like we used to and see if we can get him to talk? You like talking to the pipe, don't you? That's right, come on over and we'll have a nice talk with the pipe, just like we used to."

The paramedic sat on the ground next to the pipe and patted the ground beside him. The security guard came over and sat down.

"Okay. We'll talk to him, but we're not digging him up, no matter what he says. He's come too far to ruin it for himself now."

The paramedic looked at the black grip of the gun.

"Fine, we'll just talk," he said.

His plan was to wait for the security guard, who looked sickly and weak, to pass out or go to sleep, and then he would grab up the shovel and start digging. If the security guard didn't go to sleep within an hour or so, he planned to clobber him in the back of the head with the shovel.

Day 37

The paramedic laughed.

The supervisor had been discovered alive—turned out he had fallen asleep driving home and rolled into a slough. He had become trapped in his car, invisible from the road. Lived on packets of jelly from Hardee's for almost a week. Exhaustion and dehydration, but otherwise fine. The paramedic was off the hook.

"Do you know what I was ready to do to you last night?" he said. "I was going to lay you out, brother."

"That so?"

"Hell yeah. I was desperate, man. Way I saw it, you was standing between me and freedom. I didn't think you could keep an eye on me all night, and keep your hand on your gun the whole time, but I got to tell you. You are truly a security guard."

"That's what they pay me for."

"Whatever it is, they ain't paying you enough. Tonight I was going to slip you a mickey."

The security guard allowed himself a smile.

Day 38

The paramedic took the shift alone. The security guard had returned to work too soon, and suffered a small relapse.

About four in the morning the paramedic was asleep, dreaming about a turtle. All of a sudden the turtle opened its mouth and made a funny growling noise. The paramedic hit it with a shovel but it wouldn't quit.

He woke up. The emergency bell was going off. It sounded like an oven timer.

The paramedic knocked everything over, flailing. He grabbed the shovel and headed for the pipe. He had only struck the earth a few times when he found the problem: an electrocuted mole that had gnawed through the wire and set off the bell. The paramedic jabbed with the shovel, cutting in half both the wire and the mole. The ringing stopped.

The paramedic stood over the pipe, breathing hard.

"Hey," he said. "Can you hear me? A mole done chewed through your wire, okay? You can push that button all night long and ain't nothing going to happen. Okay? If you have a stroke or something you're just going to have to holler at me, all right? Okay? Okay then."

The paramedic put the wire back in the ground and covered it up so that it looked pretty much as it had before. He put the table and chairs back in place and opened a bottle of anisette.

Day 39

I knew our love could never get restarted
Cause every time you looked at me half-hearted

The paramedic put down the guitar.

"Now they've gone and blocked up my creativity," he said. "I can't even tell what sounds right anymore. How'd it sound to you?"

The pipe was silent.

Day 40

The security guard came back to work and he didn't look near as yellow but he was a lot quieter than before.

Day 41

"There was four of us waiting in line for the bumper cars," said the paramedic. "Me and my lady friend—not one of the ones you've met—and my brother-in-law and sister. And these kids break in line in front of us, some little runts about eight years old. So we're just like, 'Fine, kids, go ahead and break in line,' like nothing's going to happen to 'em. So the whole time, see, we're watching where the cut-off is, you know, how many people they're letting on to the bumper cars at one time. So we work it out to where we're in the same grouping as the little brats that cut ahead of us. All right? Me and my brother-in-law call ourselves the Red Team and the two gals are the Blue Team, see? That's the way we set it up. So we ganged up on those little punks and rammed the hell out of 'em. Like I'd say, 'Blue Team, go!' and they'd smash into one of these little fuckers on one side while me and the brotherman was bashing him from the other side—at the same time! It was sweet. These kids are like, 'Wah wah wah, why are the grown-ups hurting us?' And we're just like, 'Bam!' And their parents are standing on the sidelines, like 'What the hell?' I hope it was worth it, breaking in line, you fucking little punks. Those little fuckers didn't even get to drive! They spent their whole turn getting the shit rammed out of 'em! Ha ha ha!"

The security guard had no response.

Day 42

"You like oysters?"

The security guard shrugged.

"Want half my po-boy?"

"No thank you."

"I can't eat the whole thing, look at it."

"I'm all right."

"How bout some dope? Then I bet you'll eat you some po-boy. I bet you'll eat the tires off the ambulance."

"No thank you."

"You thirsty?"

"Not to speak of."

"There's something different about you since you got sick, you know that?"

"I was legally dead."

"When?"

"The other day."

"No shit."

The security guard did not elaborate.

"Well, you're alive now," said the paramedic.

"That's right," said the security guard.

"How long you dead for?"

"Couple of minutes."

"How was it?"

"It was all right."

Day 43

"The trouble with tic-tac-toe is that once you know all the moves, it's just boring. Somebody ought to invent a new kind of tic-tac-toe. Tic-tac-toe with a twist. I'm going to send that idea to myself as a registered letter and never open it. That's just as good as an official copyright. Then I'm just going to sit back and wait for some sucker to try to make money off it. I'll get right in his stupid face and whip out my envelope and say too bad, sucker! You owe me like a million dollars!"

The security guard was silent.

Day 44

"You want to race?"

"No."

"Just to the edge of that thicket and back here to the table?"

"I'd rather just sit."

"I don't believe I could have beat you before, but now I got the advantage that I never been dead."

"I don't want you talking about that anymore."

"Okay, but let me just mention one thing. I been working on my music, as you know, and I think one of the main things that's been keeping me back is I'm too uncommercialized. But if I could call the clubs and say 'I got a guy in my band that died and come back to life,' man, they'd be all over that shit. Maybe I could write a song about it and you could come and stand next to me on stage while I sung it. No big deal. Or maybe we could teach you to play drums. You'd be like the drummer that come back from the dead."

"I'm glad you got that off your chest," said the security guard. "Now I don't want to hear no more of it."

Day 45

"What's your favorite color?"

"Green."

"Really? Not blue?"

"I said green."

"Huh. Green is just a bastard of blue."

"Maybe I don't have a favorite color," said the security guard.

"Hell, man, don't go back on it. If you like green, you like green. It's none of my beeswax."

"Then why'd you ask?"

"You won't let me talk about the other thing."

The security guard shook his head.

"I understand. It's a personal matter. But you got to understand, too. It limits me to boring topics. I'm not a man that likes limits."

"I am," said the security guard.

"Hey, tomorrow's our last night. Maybe I ought to get my grandmother to pack us a big old picnic. Maybe I ought to bring my guitar and play some Steely Dan."

"I wish you wouldn't," said the security guard.

Day 46

"He's going to be a real American hero," said the paramedic, nodding at the pipe. "They're going to pull him up tomorrow morning just like a rutabaga."

The security guard didn't answer.

"I have to say, I've had worse gigs. Whole lot worse."

Still no answer.

"What are you going to do after this? Find yourself something else to guard?"

The security guard shrugged.

"Maybe a big diamond or something like that. That would be pretty cool."

"Uh-huh."

"You like those movies where there's a big diamond in a museum and five or six guys get together to steal it? One is a demolition expert and one is some other kind of expert."

"Mm."

"And they put on these all-black suits and shimmy under some laser beams to get at the diamond. Hey, I was just thinking, we should get together after this, you know. I'd like you to meet my grandmother. I bet she'd really get a kick out of you. She likes respectful people that don't talk much. She's a religious woman and you could tell her about your thing I'm not supposed to talk about. Or not. Either way. You could come over for dinner on Sunday if you want. That old lady still cooks up a storm, I mean to tell you. She can throw her down some country cooking. You like that country style cooking? You know, new potatoes and green beans, stuff like that?"

"It's all right I guess."

"She has the arthritis real bad but she still washes the dishes herself. It takes her three hours to do a sink full, and that's on a good day."

"You ought to help her."

"She won't let me. So you want to come over?"

"I don't know. I'll call you."

"You want my number? I can write it down for you."

"I'll look it up."

"You want to know what name it's under?"

"I can find out from one of the boys in payroll."

"Well, okay. We'll play it by ear."

The security guard was silent.

After awhile the paramedic said, "You want some champagne? I got some out in the ambulance."

"I'm all right," said the security guard. "You go on and drink you some if you want it."

"Man can't drink champagne by himself. That's just pitiful. You mean to tell me I went and bought champagne and you're not going to have one tee-nincey little glass?"

The security guard shook his head.

"That's all right. I'll save it for my wedding if I ever have one. They say it's better the older it gets."

"I wouldn't know."

"Hey, I got an idea. Let's you and me stick around tomorrow morning and watch 'em dig him up."

"What for?"

"I don't know. Ain't you the least bit curious? Don't you want to see the culmination of all your struggles?"

"No," said the security guard.

"Yeah," said the paramedic. "Me neither."

The security guard was silent for the rest of the shift, sitting erect and immobile in his white uniform, his yellowness faded, his skin now as pale as the pipe.

OUR SPRING CATALOG:

Upcoming Hardcover Titles
from Gurnsey & Gable Publishing

As Goes the Zephyr
by Lurleen Bivant
retail price $22.95
255 pages

This luminous and engaging first novel takes place in a suburbia unlike any suburbia you have ever encountered. Marchie Whitaker's days as a self-recriminating soccer mom and nights as an unsexed sounding board to her workaholic husband are interrupted by the surprising appearance of a rather libidinous manticore. That's just the beginning of the whimsical visitations! When workers come to dig the new swimming pool—a symbol of middle class status quo that should, *should*, answer all of Marchie's dreams, the most wonderful thing begins to happen. Goblins, trolls, witches and other inhabitants of the underworld skitter upwards through the broken soil—including the great god Pan himself! Anyway, everybody wants to lock up Marchie as a crazy person because they can't understand her magical shit. It kind of tapers off at the end, like she ran out of ideas.

I Couldn't Eat Another Thing
by Angela Bird
retail price $18.00
190 pages

In this luminous collection of sparkling stories, former newspaper columnist Bird makes a stunning fictional debut with a wry look at the state of modern commitment. A lot of the time I'd get to the end of one of the stories and turn a page like, "Huh?" Like, "Where's the end of it?" Like, "What happened next?" But nothing happened next. You know, those kind of stories. Luminous.

Low Town
by Karl Harper
retail price $24.95
361 pages

This is one of those finely wrought first novels of surprising tenderness and depth where a cool teenager is stifled by the closeminded assholes in his small town. He has sex with a lot of beautiful girls and then he makes it big as a painter and says, "So long, losers!" There's a tragedy that makes him rethink everything and pretty soon he comes of age. At the end he's headed off for fame and fortune and all the losers are sorry they didn't suck his dick when they had the chance. But in a funny kind of a way Boy Wonder will always carry a piece of Loserville with him wherever he goes. If you look at the guy's picture on the dust jacket, you'll see that he made up the part about having sex.

The Sighing of the Stones
by Louis Delmonte
retail price $24.95
400 pages

A boy and girl grope innocently toward first love against the backdrop of an Oklahoma farming community where a lot of cattle mutilations are taking place. Who cares?

The Little Dog Laughed
by Harry Parks
retail price $22.95
300 pages

Seriously, what am I doing with my life? Is this it? What am I supposed to say about this book that will make you buy it? Look at the cover. Look at the title. If you like books with covers and titles like that, go for it. It won't kill you. I keep meaning to get around to *The Naked and the Dead.*

That's supposed to be awesome. If you have to know, this particular piece of shit is about a guy who's haunted by the death of so-and-so and he takes a trip in a hot air balloon to forget all his problems. But then he finds out you can't run away from your problems. Big fucking deal.

A Good Family
by Beckinsale Cruthers
retail price $22.00
212 pages

Delia Moon had it all: riches, glamour, wit and erudition. But suddenly her Park Avenue world came crashing down around her ears. I bet you never read a book like this before! It's about the horrible pain and turmoil of being rich and white. The Moon family has a shitload of dramatic tragedies and problems. I think there's some incest in there. That makes the title ironic! *Kirkus Reviews* is going to eat this shit up.

The Enormous Swan
by M. A. McCorquedale
retail price $30.00
650 pages

Set against the colorful backdrop of some historical period nobody gives a rat's ass about, *The Enormous Swan* tells the story of a humble craftsman who comes into contact with an emperor or some shit. To tell you the truth I didn't make it past page 10. It's one of those books where the author spent half his life in a library looking up facts about medieval culinary techniques and galley slaves and shit, and now he thinks we're supposed to care.

Eat the Lotus
by Marie Overstreet
retail price $22.00
241 pages

I swear to God I'm going to cut my own throat. I just don't give a shit. Husband and wife reach a crossroads in their relationship against the colorful backdrop of blah blah blah. They're haunted by the suicide of their only son. Pull yourself together you pussies! God I'm sick of this shit. I'd rather work at fucking McDonald's, I swear to God. You know what? It's not even about my career goals anymore. "Come on, Annie, this job will be good experience. You'll make a lot of contacts. I want to read your novel, Annie. When am I going to get to see this novel of yours, Annie?" You can bite my ass, you creepy old fuck. One day you're going to get what's coming to you.

SO THIS IS WRITING!

Episode One: The Poet I Know

1

The poet is pregnant.

I keep saying, "You should name the baby after me." I say, "It's a good name for a boy or a girl." I say a lot of other things.

I'm not serious am I?

My buddy Hodge likes to tell me I'm a bit self-absorbed, but I don't know. I ponder it all the time.

For example, the poet puts her friends' names in her poems. I keep thinking, when is she going to put me in a poem?

Like how about the time we saw that sunset?

Is that self-absorbed?

Of course I was drunk and I talked all the way through the sunset.

Like, "Look at that!"

Like, "Wow!"

Like, "I think I saw a fish!"

The poet said, because the sun was a fierce dot above the bay, casting a rope of fire toward us on the water, "An exclamation point."

I said, "I was just going to say that!"

I said, "I was going to say a Spanish exclamation point!"

I said, "Because it's upside down!"

The sun plunged all of a sudden and you could feel the temperature drop just as the poet had predicted.

What had happened that day?

Let me start over.

Hodge and I had been out of work for some time. We decided to become writers. We were getting old and as long as our lives were in shambles what did we have to lose? We thought, "It's now or never."

I called the poet's husband to ask him how to become a writer.

"Well, you could start by going to some of these conferences," said the poet's husband.

The poet's husband and I had been friends since early childhood. He had become a famous novelist. He was my "contact."

Hodge and I drove down to the Conference of Southern Authors. Our wives stayed behind.

We went to the opening night reading.

First there was a story about a guy who drank too much and harbored bad thoughts about himself. He had one last shot to make good.

Somebody else read about the marvelous and eventful tea party that Mrs. Magnolia P. Dillblossom threw for her rebellious daughter Topsy.

Then came a tale where everybody had names like "T-Toe" and "Little Jay Joe" and "Moedine" and slept in pick-up trucks with dogs and chickens and talked about their "britches" and so on.

Well, Hodge and I kept nudging each other. So this was writing! Writing was going to be a piece of cake!

"What are your influences?" somebody asked the panel.

Everybody said Faulkner.

I wrote in my notebook: "Read Faulkner."

The next day we got there early. Listless, bent writers decorated the lawn of the converted church where the next reading would be held. It wasn't noon by a long shot but some of the writers clearly cradled beer in plastic cups. It seemed appealing.

I introduced Hodge to the poet's husband.

"Where can we get a beer?" I said. "Or is that just for writers?"

"Come on," said the poet's husband. "We'll go to the bar where I lost my coat last night."

We headed for the car.

"Will we be back in time for the reading?" I said.

"They can't start without me," said the poet's husband. "I need to find my coat anyway. Either I lost it or __________ stole it." (He named a certain drunken writer.)

We drove around the corner to a little shack that smelled like fish. All the doors were open so things were lit that shouldn't have been lit. Stools, forlorn, showed their pale stuffing, for example. Tin and concrete everywhere, startled by the sun. There was just room for Hodge, the poet's husband and myself at the small bar, at the end of which a sulky stranger stood drinking.

"Did anybody turn in a coat last night?" the poet's husband asked the woman tending bar.

"Is this it?" she said, holding up a coat.

"No, it was a nice coat."

"What's a nice coat? Nobody turned in a nice coat. You wouldn't happen to be _______, would you?"

To our surprise, she named the same drunken writer to whom the poet's husband had recently alluded.

"Yes, that's me, why do you ask?" said the poet's husband.

The bartender handed him an American Express gold card.

"This isn't really me," said the poet's husband. "I know him, though. I was here last night, remember? I was in here with him."

The bartender looked doubtful.

"I'm about to see him in fifteen minutes. I tell you what, put a round of drinks on this card. He won't mind. He's a sweet man. Buy a drink for that guy, too." He pointed to the end of the bar.

The sulky stranger brightened.

"Hey," he said.

The bartender looked doubtful.

"Come on, he's a sweet man. He'd want to reward us for finding his card. We're friends of his. Remember, he was making up songs? He was really funny? Another guy was playing guitar?"

"That's right," said the bartender.

"Come on, one round of drinks. I'll sign for him. He's a sweet man."

She said okay.

We all ordered drinks and had a great laugh.

The poet's husband fingered the gold card. "I ought to buy a coat with this," he said. He handed the card to me. "You hang on to it. I might buy a coat with it."

I put the card in my shirt pocket.

I must say that an extremely pleasant ten minutes followed, among the most pleasant imaginable. Hodge and I discussed our aspirations with a real writer, a true friend, who seemed to have faith in us. We laughed and drank free beer in an atmosphere of unprecedented trust and generosity, where a bartender was knowingly letting us use another person's credit card without permission, and we had made a stranger's day. The stranger wasn't the least bit sulky anymore! The bartender stirred a cauldron of rich-smelling gumbo. The day had a buzz. We hated to do it, but finally we had to go back to the church.

A couple of flat-eyed tough guy writers stood on the piney lawn, near the breezeway that led to the former chapel. They were taking turns drinking from a flask. The writing life was just as I had imagined it! I could easily picture Hodge and myself in a similar position, swapping a flask of rye or such back and forth in a casual manner out in the open for all to see without a care in the world. I wrote in my notebook:

"2. Buy flask."

I nudged Hodge and showed it to him. He grinned.

"What you got there?" said the poet's husband.

"Nothing," I said, and closed the notebook quickly. Suddenly I had become ashamed of my grand aspirations!

The poet's husband introduced us to the craggy novelist and the drunken writer.

"I've seen your picture in the newspaper," I told the craggy novelist.

"Thanks," he said.

"Has it started?" asked the poet's husband.

"Yeah, but if you go in now be sure to take your estrogen supplement."

The craggy novelist and drunken writer snickered.

I took it that some women were reading, and that their writing was insufficiently masculine.

"Hey, we found your credit card," said the poet's husband.

I took the card from my shirt pocket and handed it to the drunken writer. Somehow he got it into his head that I alone had been responsible for rescuing his credit card, and he hugged me over and over. He was smiling and making snappy jokes but there was something aggressive about the hugging and his stubble burned my face.

The poet's husband, the craggy novelist and the drunken writer used a special entrance. Hodge and I stood in the back of the church for the reading, in what would have been, in more sacred times, the narthex.

"__________ is pretty funny, isn't he?" I whispered to Hodge.

"I think he's dangerous. He strikes me as the type of guy that can be funny and then suddenly turn on you."

"Maybe," I said.

"Stay away from him," said Hodge.

There were readings by the poet, and the poet's husband, and the craggy novelist. Well, they put Hodge and me in our place! Writing no longer seemed like a breeze. The things that came out of their mouths! The air was heavy with reality, that's all. They grabbed reality and ran a fire along the bumpy surface—or showed the red meat under the skin, like when you clap your hand over a flashlight. Writing seemed like a hard job, an impossible job for the likes of Hodge and me. Middle-aged men! Starting from scratch!

We returned to the sunlight humbled, and drank more beer in the breezeway. There were three or four coolers of it, just lying around like nothing. Pretty soon it was time for all the writers to go to a party at the home of a patroness of the arts, a certain Mrs. Post. The poet and her husband said that Hodge and I should come along.

"Are you sure?"

"Free food."

We ended up right on the water, in a mansion jammed full of screaming writers, professors, mavens, hoydens and such. I thought I saw some tycoons. Movers and shakers. Ne'er-do-wells and pillars of the community. Social butterflies. Maybe even a pariah. We walked around in the backyard with bottles of beer and paper plates full of curries and pastas and rare roast beef with horseradish on the side and chicken salad with apples and walnuts and other catered foods. People were falling down drunk. You could hear, clearly, through the din, the drunken writer roughly cawing, loud as a bullhorn, cutting through everything like his famous knifelike prose.

The sun began to look as though it might want to set.

The poet asked her husband, "Do you want to walk down to the end of the pier and watch the sunset?"

"Fuck no," said her husband. "Fuck the sunset."

"That reminds me of a James Thurber cartoon," I said. I tried unsuccessfully to explain what I was talking about.

"You're going to miss a beautiful sunset," said the poet.

"Seen one you've seen them all," said her husband.

"I'll go with you," I said.

"Thank you," said the poet.

We headed for the pier.

"Sunsets are for pussies," her husband called.

2

Hodge and I kind of wanted to hit the road after the party, but we went back to the church instead because the drunken writer was going to read, and he was supposed to be hilarious. His book had a hilarious title.

The program was delayed while different authorities tried to find the drunken writer and force him on stage. Finally he crawled up of his own free will and read a story very slowly with lots of odd pauses. Many times we could not understand what he was saying. Other times he would yell out, for no apparent reason, "Thank you, George W. Bush!" Even with all that going on, the story was funny and we laughed upon several occasions.

Hodge and I sneaked out before the next writer started. The church lawn was black and eerie in the dim electric light. On our way to the parking lot we found the poet alone in the dark, on a bench, eyes shut, head drooping. She wore an air of distress!

"Are you okay?" I said.

She shook her head.

"Is there anything I can do?"

She shook her head.

"Is everything all right?"

She shook her head.

"Can I get you something?"

She shook her head.

"Okay," I said. "Are you sure you don't need anything?"

"Thank you, I'm fine," she said.

Hodge and I got in the car and drove away.

"I hope she's all right," I said.

"She's pretty," said Hodge.

"Uh-huh."

"You sure were on that pier a long time," Hodge said.

"What's that supposed to mean?" I said.

"Oh, nothing."

"It takes a long time for the sun to go down."

"Sure it does."

"Well, it does!"

"I know, I'm agreeing with you."

"Well, then, what are you getting at?"

"I don't know. I thought she looked sad."

"Sad how?"

"Like she and her husband had had a fight."

"Really?"

"Yeah."

"About...? No!"

"Okay then."

"You really think...?"

"All I'm saying is, you were out on that pier for a long time."

"What? So what? That's his wife! He's my oldest friend, one of the best friends I've ever had! And what about Happy?" (Happy is my wife.)

"Don't tell me, tell him."

"Oh, he wouldn't think... He's the nicest person in the world."

"Fine, then, it's settled. Settled to the satisfaction of all! She was sitting all alone in the dark for no reason. Case closed."

"Maybe she was tired."

"A man and a woman at the end of the pier. Watching the sun sink slowly into the ocean. Alone. Makes a real pretty picture. Real pretty."

"Would you shut up?"

"Oh, don't mind me. Case closed. Nicest person in the world. Oldest friend for many years."

"Well, you know, he can get really jealous."

"Yeah?"

"Well, he's been known to get jealous. Yeah, like one time I walked through the mall with this girl he liked and he got so mad he snapped his pen in two and got ink all over himself."

"Hmm."

I was quiet for a long time.

Hodge started laughing.

"What?"

"What do I always tell you?"

"Oh!"

I started laughing too. Right! The self-absorbed thing.

Turns out it's true!

I want my name in poems. I want people, all people, to name their babies after me. I imagine myself to cut such a dashing figure on the dusky pier, even as a distant silhouette, that I cause great rifts in the solid marriages of my most beloved friends. Me with my eczema!

Hodge sure had "my number." Yes, the joke was "on me." This I knew at once, even before finding out the next day that the poet had been, after all, just terribly ill with a surfeit of drink (I hasten to add that this incident did not occur during her pregnancy).

Hodge and I laughed for awhile and then we stopped laughing.

"That's quite an imagination you have," I said.

"You're highly suggestible," said Hodge.

"Yes, between the two of us we're going to make a good writer."

SO THIS IS WRITING!

Episode Two: The Consultants

1

Hodge thought his brother was full of crap. I was more optimistic.

Hodge thought it was strange that his brother had offered to pay us for "standing around holding clipboards and looking official." Hodge said it reeked of scam.

I preferred to think of it as a favor. Hodge and I had been out of work for a long time, and our plans to turn into famous writers had not yet borne fruit. I told Hodge not to be a pessimist. Yes, his brother was throwing us a bone out of sheer pity. Yes, we would probably come back from our trip a thousand bucks in the hole, despite the per diem that Hodge's brother had generously offered to provide. Yes, there was something fishy about the whole deal. Say it was a scam. Well, even that scam might lead to something else, thanks to the environment we were about to enter, hanging out with bigshots and somebodys in nightspots and boardrooms. And if the project was on the up-and-up, we'd be in on the ground floor! We had a chance to show Hodge's brother that we were the real McCoys, creative and energetic. Young at heart with lots of big ideas.

I don't fly because of my personal problems. I took it as a good sign that Hodge's brother forked over for a train ticket right away, no grousing, though we had never met nor even spoken. He used his "corporate credit card" to put me up in my very own sleeper, a little bonus that made me like him even more. Hodge thought I was a big jerk for not flying like him. I told him to sue me for loving America. Hodge asked me what getting hemorrhoids sitting my ass on a train for nineteen hours had to do with loving America and I couldn't explain it but I knew in my heart. "You're the exact opposite of your brother," I told Hodge. Hodge said that I didn't know his brother and should keep my mouth shut about things I didn't know. I appraised him silently.

2

All aboard!

My sleeper was as cozy as could be. And my meals in the elegant dining car were included in the price of the ticket! Another fringe benefit, thanks to Hodge's brother.

I was seated for dinner with an older couple. The man said he was an environmental engineer. I felt pleased to mention that I was on my way to help "pitch" a television show to Fame – The Channel, and the couple was delighted to speak to me about it. Their tired old skin became rosy and sparkling. In response to my exciting business dealings the woman, her hair bottle-red, said with evident disdain, "*My* son is a tattoo artist in Louisville, Kentucky. Have you been to Louisville?"

"It's a big industrial town," said her husband. "UPS and KFC."

"I've been to Paducah," I said. "The way I came in it looked like nothing but bowling alleys and liquor stores."

"That's Kentucky to a T," said Red.

"It was probably just the way I came into town," I said.

"No it wasn't. Have you ever heard of someone making a living as a tattoo artist?"

"Lots of people make money that way," said the husband.

"At forty years old?"

"Well I don't see why not. He has a nice car."

"How will he ever get a decent job with those things all over his body?"

"Oh, they can remove them now. It's very painful."

"I think I read that they buried a lot of nuclear waste in Paducah back in the fifties," I told the husband.

I thought he might be able to confirm it, being an environmental engineer and all. He just sort of looked at me.

"I think they called it the Atomic City," I said. "They were proud of it. I think they put it on postcards. Welcome to Paducah – the Atomic City. I guess they're not so proud now! Hey! I just thought of something. Now you have to understand, I come from a little shrimping town called Pleasant Progress. When my little brother was about twelve he drew a fake postcard that said 'Welcome to Pleasant Progress – A Great Place to Paint a

Boat.'"I laughed. "Huh. I don't know why I suddenly remembered that."

"We live near a famous Spanish Mission," said the husband.

"San Luis Obispo, California. We just love it. We haven't moved in thirty-six years," Red added.

"Wow! That's where she falls off the tower in *Vertigo*, isn't it?"

The husband laughed with wan, mellow rue. "No, I'm afraid that honor goes to San Juan Bautista. The grounds at least. The actual tower is somewhere else, I believe. But our mission is famous too. Even if no movie stars saw fit to grace it."

"San Juan Bautista. My wife would kill me," I said. "She's an expert on Hitchcock."

They didn't seem to care. That was okay. I guess it's not too exciting to hear what other people's relatives are experts at.

I had noticed that the woman said "*We've*" been in San Luis Obispo for 36 years, but "*My*" son is a tattoo artist. People sure have intricate lives! I made a mental note to jot that down on a piece of paper.

My new friends were thrilled to find sweet potato pie on the dessert menu.

"Oprah!" said the husband.

"Oprah says sweet potato pie is her favorite dessert. She talks about it all the time," Red explained. "Have you ever had it?"

"I sure have," I said.

"What's it like?"

"It's good. Not much different than pumpkin pie."

"We should get it!"

They threw caution to the wind. Afterward the husband said, "Now we can say we've eaten what Oprah eats!"

3

Hodge and I climbed aboard a roomy, rolling silver escalator that was kind of like the escalator to Heaven. St. Peter stood at the top, a guard who kept crazy people from getting into the cove of elevators behind him. Some people passed by, flashing ID badges.

Hodge fished around for the extension of the person who was supposed to help us. The guard punched it in but couldn't raise a soul. Hodge asked him to try it again.

"In a minute," he said. He let some people through, and then he let some more people through.

"Can you try that extension again?" Hodge said. "It's *Boy Oh Paperboy*?"

The guard said he'd never heard of it.

"Yeah, well, it's a situation comedy? They're rehearsing upstairs somewhere."

"They're doing a lot of things upstairs," the guard said.

We weren't dressed appropriately, and—discounting the guard and the man shining shoes in the lobby—we were clearly the oldest people in the building. I fear that I lost my self-respect and stopped admiring myself for who I was. I saw us as I imagined the smooth young bunch saw us: a premature geezer with skunk hair (Hodge) and his fatso chum with the brown teeth (me).

"Come on, we'll try again later," I said.

"We'll be back, Charlie," Hodge said to the guard. "You can count on that."

The guard was unflustered.

4

I am afraid we started drinking. There are bars everywhere in New York! We walked right into one where they had free burnt popcorn. I told them to keep the Guinnesses coming.

Every once in awhile I would suggest that it might be time to go back and try again. Hodge just said, "Nah." Or he said something about his brother disrespecting him. Or he said, "We did our part." Or, "If he wants us so bad he can come and find us."

We went to the bar at our hotel and Hodge insisted upon charging a few rounds of salty dogs to his brother's room. Pretty soon we were in quite a state. I no longer mentioned going back to the Fame – The Channel building, for it was no longer a smart idea.

We had lunch in a homey Italian place. I enjoyed a bottle of wine.

Evening found us in a fancier restaurant, where we sat under a movie poster from the 1920s.

"They don't make 'em like that anymore," said Hodge, nodding at the poster. "I guess that monkey is in love with the girl."

"And he's a cop," I said. "That's nuts. Wait a minute. Holy cow, I don't believe it. That's supposed to be an Irishman!"

"No..." said Hodge, but he looked again and had to agree. "Well..."

Yes the redfaced stub-nosed cartoon monkey was supposed to be an Irishman with a filthy orange mane of a beard.

"I guess it makes sense," said Hodge. "Why would a monkey be dressed as a policeman, and in love with a regular woman? I mean, he's in love with her, right? Look at that look on his face. Like some love-crazed monkey."

"That's what they thought Irishmen looked like," I said. "Like big ugly redheaded monkeys."

By the time I was on my second ginger-and-lemon infused grappa, it occurred to me that the name of the restaurant, Thalia, was also the name of the Greek muse of comedy. "It's a good omen," I kept saying. "Don't you think it's a good omen?"

Hodge didn't seem to care so I snagged the waiter.

"Hey," I said. "Hey, hey, excuse me. Thalia? That's the Greek muse of comedy, right?"

"Yes sir."

"See? I told you!" I screamed. Hodge just looked at me.

"I told him!" I said to the waiter. "Hey, do you work tomorrow night?"

"Are you thinking of coming back?"

"We're going to come here every night! This place is great!"

"I'm glad you're enjoying yourself."

"I sure am!"

"Another grappa?"

"Yeah, let me try the one with the rosemary in it, or whatever it was."

"Very good, sir."

"He was just telling you that," said Hodge.

"What?"

"The muse of comedy or whatever. He wants a tip. He's telling you anything you want to hear."

5

The next day I felt pretty lousy. Hodge and I were up in Central Park, in a daze. We met a squat, happy, redfaced horse-and-buggy man who wanted to be our best friend when we boasted to him about our TV dealings. The horse-and-buggy man had written a script about a heroic horse-and-buggy man who saves New York City from a disaster by racing through the city on his horse and buggy. An international crisis has caused the ultimate traffic jam in the streets of New York. The horse-and-buggy man didn't want to give too much away, suffice it to say that a certain object needs to be in the hands of a certain person at a certain time, and thanks to his knowledge of the city's geography, and his extraordinary skills as a driver and an equestrian, only the hero can deliver it.

He said he would have shown the script to us, but he had promised "first look" to the starlet Jennifer Love Hewitt, who had ridden in his buggy one day. He had told her there was a part she was perfect for, a hot actress who fell in love with the horse-and-buggy man. The actress is engaged to one of these Wall Street a-holes who treats her like crap, but she doesn't really love him. Her family is forcing them to get married. After the horse-and-buggy man saves the city, the actress's snooty family has to admit he's just as good as the Wall Street a-hole. Then the actress jumps his bones. It was a strong part for a woman, something sorely lacking in today's Hollywood.

We told our new friend goodbye and headed down to the building to take another shot at getting in.

Hodge kind of puffed up at the guard—in vain, for he didn't remember us. Anyway, it didn't matter; this time we managed to get someone to come down: a thin, worried, grinning lad in a backward baseball cap.

"*Boy Oh Paperboy*?" he said.

We nodded.

"They're with me," he told the guard. I can't speak for Hodge, but I have to say I swelled with pride! An escort! Express elevator, all the way to the top! We waltzed right in, past a number of fidgety souls who found themselves barred in the same hopeless way we had been the day before. I should not have taken such pleasure in their failings, having recently been in their very shoes, but I am not a perfect man.

As we neared the executive lounge, which the intern (for so the lad was) told us had been transformed into a makeshift staging area, we were met by the woozy, transporting smell of frying breakfast. They had a jolly aproned lady making omelets—just to mention one item—on demand! For free!

In the "wings," actors (no one I recognized) studied their scripts or chatted with pretty young women who seemed to have important jobs. Some of the younger actors shot pool, bright balls clacking on crimson felt. There was an air of camaraderie!

"That would be a pretty good job," I said to Hodge, nodding at the young men playing their game. "This is more like recess than a job. I guess anything goes in show business, apparently!"

Hodge agreed. But then he had to turn the jollity into bitterness as usual, observing: "Leave it to my brother to get into a lazy-ass racket like this."

I suggested that Hodge should track down his brother in the hubbub, but Hodge seemed ambivalent. Family relationships can be complex!

Believe it or not, we got into a conversation with a celebrity lookalike who had written a script about a celebrity lookalike. This guy, Brad, was supposed to look like Eddie Murphy, and he did, sort of. In Brad's idea, Eddie Murphy decides to rob a bank, wearing no disguise or anything, because he knows it will confuse the witnesses and nobody will ever believe that Eddie Murphy would rob a bank. The perfect crime! The only reason that Eddie Murphy robs the bank is that he is bored with being a star and having everything handed to him on a platter. There are no thrills left for him! He can have everything he wants yet he wants more. So anyway he robs the bank and the crime is pinned on an innocent Eddie Murphy lookalike who happens to have a juvie record. Now the lookalike must pull off the greatest performance of his career, tracking down the real culprit… Eddie Murphy himself!

The twist, Brad explained, was that the lookalike (Brad) would play Eddie Murphy and Eddie Murphy would play the lookalike.

Hodge said, "Yeah, but wouldn't it be cooler if Eddie Murphy just played both parts?"

Brad went away.

Among the many actors were half a dozen lookalikes: Eddie Murphy, Billy Idol, Bill Clinton, Nathan Lane, Glen Campbell and Bob Balaban. They served as placeholders for the real-life stars who had been written into the script, and who were supposed to play themselves if the pilot ever got off the ground. Hodge and I cracked a lot of jokes about the Bob Balaban impersonator. We said this was probably the first job he had ever gotten. Then we decided that maybe he really *was* Bob Balaban. Wouldn't that be something?

Hodge said, "Hey, here's a pretty good idea for a movie. An out-of-work actor achieves more success as his own lookalike than he ever did as himself."

"And learns something about himself in the process?"

"Not necessarily."

"But he meets a girl," I suggested. "He falls in love with the *lookalike* of a lead actress he once had a crush on. Then, when she finds out he's the real Bob Balaban, or whoever, and that he used to be in love with the actress she *looks* like, it causes all kinds of hurt feelings and misunderstandings. But then he convinces her that he loves what's on the inside. The name of the movie is *Lookalike Love*. No, *Looks Like Love*. No, *Love-alike*."

"Too predictable."

I was starting to think that Hodge was going "Hollywood." He was dismissive of my creative input. Maybe he was showing off, trying to be part of the "in" crowd. Maybe he had some big ideas.

I went back to the hotel and lay down, ill from my shenanigans of the day before and rather sensitively angry with Hodge, I grieve to admit. In my reverie I imagined myself becoming friends with Hodge's interesting and successful brother over the course of the week. I imagined that he might take a liking to my personality and hire me to do some eccentric errands, perhaps as his professional dinner companion—I'd be paid just for eating!—or perhaps as his personal private investigator.

I was jarred by the sound of Hodge pounding on my door. I jumped up and let him in. He was in a rage.

Hodge told me to pack my bags, we were "out of here." It turned out that Hodge had "pitched" his brother an idea for another show, and

Hodge's brother had shrugged him off, even though it was a million times better than *Boy Oh Paperboy*.

"What was it?" I asked.

Hodge wouldn't say.

I wanted to ask if Hodge's brother had specified that I should leave too, but I kept mum instead, out of loyalty, I guess. I even had to *fly* back because of the hasty arrangements. It seemed like a punishment for something. Hubris, maybe. Like Icarus of ancient lore!

6

Now that I'm back, my wife Happy and I go to the movies during the day, sometimes two in a row. I guess it's pretty dumb, but before I left for the trip I encouraged Happy to quit her miserable job. She did. She has applied to a couple of doctorate programs already, but there hasn't been any news, and I still don't have a job, so everything is up in the air. I suppose I had misrepresented *Boy Oh Paperboy* as a sure thing. I had been guilty of clinging to vaporous dreams. I have sunk us, I suppose, into a fiscal and spiritual quagmire for which there seems no solace. I have lied, as people do, to both my spouse and myself.

We went to this one movie where they showed a chimpanzee stick his finger in his butt and then he sniffed his finger and the smell was so bad it made him fall off his tree branch.

You could tell it hadn't been faked like most stuff in the movies, someone had accidentally caught it on camera and it was so funny that they just had to use it.

When that monkey fell out of the tree I laughed so hard I started crying, crying real streams, and I really thought for sure my heart would seize up and I would die. I felt hot all over. I could tell I was distracting other moviegoers but I couldn't stop shrieking. That's what I was doing. Shrieking. I guess I missed ten whole minutes of the movie that way.

When we were driving home I said, humorously but accurately, and in a measured voice, "I don't think you understand. A monkey put its finger in its butt. Then it sniffed its finger. And the smell was *so bad* it literally knocked the monkey out of the tree."

"Uh-huh," said Happy.

Two days later we were in line at the grocery store. I started laughing.

"What?" said Happy.

"I was just thinking about that monkey."

ATTENTION JOHNNY AMERICA! PLEASE READ!

I am sending this to your publication of __________ and I hope that you will print it. I cannot afford to pay for it as an advertisement of blank amount per word. There is a subject that everyone is talking about today, and that is Johnny America. He is the mysterious crusader who has sprung forth from our imaginations much like a colorful character in a comic book so they say. But as everyone knows he is for real 100%. I have seen his costume up close and it appears to be blue shiny and scaly. I am only mentioning certain details to lend myself credibility. Why am I writing, is to explain that Johnny America has made a mistake about me personally and to make a public statement that I would like him to leave me alone. That is not to scorn any of the great things he has done for our community. But isn't it possible that anyone can make a mistake. That is all I am saying.

I have been out of work because some logs fell on my leg. The doctor says I should move around somewhat. In the past I have enjoyed walking to the grocery store and purchasing some things to make for dinner. When my wife came home she was pleased to find the smell of cooking in the house and it made me feel like I was contributing some thoughtfulness to our relationship.

On one such day I was returning from the store with two bags of groceries when who should spring out of nowhere but Johnny America, who I did not know it was him at the time, just some gaudy dressed person who looked exciting to me, like there was a parade or celebration nearby.

He told me that I was very clever but one day I was going to slip up. Then he hit me in the stomach very hard causing me to drop my groceries and kneel on the ground in great pain, also landing on my bad knee.

I was made aware that this was the real Johnny America for to my surprise blue flames shot out from beneath his cape and he flew amazingly to the top of a neighboring building and scampered agilely away.

My reaction was bewildered. For a long time I was scared to get off the ground.

Needless to say I did not cook dinner but sat in the apartment trying to figure all the ways I might have made Johnny America upset. Some awful things raced through my mind, things I have done that I am not proud of. Talking a lot when I am drunk in a blaring and inconsiderate manner. I also have greed and sloth and many other unlikable qualities.

When my wife arrived home I told her my tale. She became agitated and threatened to put an announcement on the telephone poles of our neighborhood, warning of vigilante activity as she called it. She began to draw one such object, displaying the talent as an artist she had exercised in college. The stinging sarcasm of her wording and drawing caused me to become alarmed. I did not wish for the boat to be rocked where Johnny America was concerned. My wife expressed it as me taking a beating and thanking the beater for the privilege. In a rude manner I snatched her paper away and tore it into many ribbons. There were other ways I could have expressed myself better without violence and censorship. This led to a terrible argument. There were many recriminations. We got so tired of arguing that it actually put us to sleep.

Exactly one week and one day after my first adventure I again encountered Johnny America in the same surprising manner. I was dismayed for he seemed purposeful and his face was stern.

I thought I told you to stay out of this area, he said. Decent people live here, he went on. He emphasized the word decent as if to imply that I was not decent. I had no groceries at the time to drop, being on the way to the store rather than coming from it, but he harshly blackened my eye explaining that he would give me something to remember him by. Once again I was preempted from clearing my name by seeing him blast off in a cloud of amazing blue flame.

This night I cooked dinner as usual and made as if all was well. My bruise I explained by saying that my bad knee had buckled and I had stricken my head upon the divan. My wife was solicitous and we had a pleasant evening. That night there was a televised report that Johnny America had stopped a gas leak in a shopping mall just before it was about to blow up numerous innocent people. I could not reveal the complicated nature of my thoughts, which were, How can a man so good and true act in a manner so mistaken where I am concerned. All those people whose life he saved tonight could not care less if he gets it wrong about one man, so ran my troubling thoughts. If he killed me even, I continued to think, would everyone believe that Johnny America knew best. Apart from my wife I tried to imagine others who would rally to my side and there were none that I could think of right away, a fact that filled me with emotions.

One night I awoke to see Johnny America climbing into our bedroom window. He held a rag over the face of my sleeping wife. I suppose it was chloroform to prevent her from awakening from the beating he then gave me. He took me to the kitchen, dragging me along by pinching my neck in an uncomfortable manner. He wrapped two small potatoes and a lemon in a dishrag and hit me on the chest, stomach, back and buttocks area several times in a harsh manner. Without a word he left me lying on the floor. I do not know if he again sped away on a chariot of blue flame but I suspect such was the case.

My wife did not believe my tale of what had happened. The manner of beating had been constructed as I now believe so as not to produce bruising upon my body and therefore to further discredit me. The ironical thing of it was that now my wife seemed to doubt anything I had said about Johnny America at all. When I mentioned my blackened eye as evidence she referred scoffingly to the divan.

Please do not print my name or current location, which is not my usual home. I cannot afford to stay here too much longer. I can no longer sleep with any success. My wife is with a distant relative of hers whose relationship and name I shall not mention for safety. Things are not going too well with us. I do not blame Johnny America for that, or for anything else for he is just doing his job and my marital problems are of my own making. Maybe Johnny America has done me a favor by bringing to my attention an atmosphere of marital discomfort that has been boiling beneath the surface all along. I cannot blame him for that! In fact I should thank him! My only request is that he will place a personal ad in this publication that announces his intention not to beat me any more. If you mention what was in my grocery bags that first time you knocked me down, I will know for sure it is you.

In conclusion thank you for your many efforts on behalf of the community. Good luck with your future endeavors. You have my support 100% Johnny America!

DEAR *PEOPLE* MAGAZINE, KEEP UP THE GREAT CYCLOPS COVERAGE

for Jamie Kornegay and Don Novello

Oh say can you see? I'll say I can! The Cyclops gives a new meaning to "Old Glory" as he inspires the troops in a bellybutton-revealing replica of the stars and stripes. Thank you, *People*, for reminding us in these troubled times that there are still legendary monsters who take the time out to let our brave boys in uniform know how a grateful nation feels. *This* Cyclops can keep his eye on me anytime!

*

The photo of the Cyclops "whooping it up" on the back of a motorcycle is priceless! Thank you, *People*, for an image that is sure to become a cherished memory—at least on *this* reader's refrigerator! From now on I'll be keeping "one eye open"... for the Cyclops, that is!

*

It saddens me to read of the Cyclops "feeling blue." I guess longtime friend Sean Penn hit the nail on the head when he was quoted as saying that the Cyclops is "fragile." As fragile as a baby bird, I might add. But a whole lot sexier! Is it just me, or do I detect a cry for help behind that supposedly menacing one-eyed stare? It is almost as if the Cyclops is saying, "Hold me, understand me." Who has not felt such urges in these trying times? Penn goes on to say that the Cyclops can be "really funny" and then turn around and be "very shy." Who can understand such a bundle of complex contradictions? I for one would like to try.

*

Add another color to those patriotic stripes of red white and blue—that's right, coppery green. For just such a becoming shade of green is the color of the Cyclops when he disguises himself as the Statue of Liberty and lets the public take his picture for charitable purposes. Thank you, *People* magazine, for one in a series of remarkable profiles in courage. It is refreshing to find a cherished few who are not ashamed to drape themselves in the flag—literally! Hats off, Cyclops! Or should I say "Crowns off"? "Eye" salute you! Yearning to breathe free, indeed. And a breath of fresh air he is.

*

Sorry, ladies! The Cyclops is off the market. That's the message of your recent delightful article "The Cyclops Has an Eye on Marriage." On a more subdued note, surely who amongst us can begrudge the Cyclops the happiness he deserves after many personal tragedies. It saddens me, however, to note that his handsome young nephews may not attend the wedding. Surely they understand that some things are more important than riches and polo matches—and among those things are the simple joys of family. Here's hoping they "open their eyes" to love.

*

Of all the celebrities you have ever profiled, perhaps the most intriguing is a one-eyed giant. I am referring of course to the Cyclops. One quibble: Why bury the Cyclops at the back of your magazine? With his rakish hat, smoldering scowl and ever-present cigar (not to mention the sly twinkle in his large and intriguing eye) he can hold his own against a whole gaggle of Hollywood pretty boys any day of the week. And oh yeah… He just happens to be the Cyclops! But that is a small complaint indeed given your excellent coverage of a "truly classic monster," as Cyclops fan Abe Plumpton so ably puts it in the article in question. Whether winning a Nobel Prize in Literature, sipping his beloved scotch or watching his father die of syphilis, "Ol' One Eye" has always known how to handle even the toughest situation with grace and style. Perhaps in this time of national crisis, that remains the most important lesson of all.

THE GOLDEN PINEAPPLES

One squirrel sat in the hollow of a tree, staring at Mitch as he raked. This squirrel, with its particularly pious and sullen air, reminded Mitch of Harriet Scott, one of the persons who had ruined him. A second squirrel, the one Mitch referred to as "Gibson," loved to perch on the stubby knot of another tree.

"He even has a head like Gibson's," Mitch told Jenny. "Remember Gibson's head?"

Gibson's big round head had expanded whenever he drank alcohol. People bought him stingers just to see it happen. Gibson did crazy, mean things like collecting the paper dots from the hole puncher until he had a whole pail of them, and then he'd dump it on somebody's head. For some reason everyone loved him.

Gibson had engineered Mitch's layoff while smiling to his face.

It was mildly eerie, the way the squirrels showed up and glued themselves to the exact same observation posts *every time* Mitch picked up the rake. Mitch said, half aloud, to the squirrels, all the things he *should have* said to the jerks who had robbed him of his dignity, all the terrifying, gory threats he should have made to the people whose fingers he would have liked to smash in car doors, whose faces he would have liked to spit in while everyone was watching and cheering, who he should have pushed down stairs, whose loved ones he would have liked to call on the phone and frighten with awful imaginary stories about death.

Still, raking was kind of an improvement. Before that he had stayed in the attic, watching a TV with no picture, just sound.

Mitch and Jenny had been planning to refurbish the attic, turn it into a cool livable area. All that had stopped with the layoff. Mitch didn't have the energy, for one thing. So the attic had been refurbished just enough to make it barren and depressing. It smelled like sawdust. There was a scarred blonde desk in one corner, nothing on it but a plastic frog covered in lime green felt. The frog was smoking a red-tipped plastic cigar and holding a sign that said, "DON'T SMOKE OR I MIGHT CROAK."

Mitch thought about that frog a lot.

It had graced his desk at work. He had asked almost everyone who had come by his cubicle to check out the frog. Usually there was no initial reaction.

Mitch would say, "Look again."

Nothing, usually.

"Think about it."

"What am I supposed to be seeing?"

"He's telling *you* not to smoke or he might croak, but..."

Mitch and his visitor would share a good laugh.

"He doesn't want *you* to smoke..."

"... but he has a huge cigar in his mouth!"

"He's doing the very thing that makes him fear for his life!"

"That frog is crazy!"

"He should worry about his own bad habits before chiding others, am I right? Are you with me?"

"Yeah! What kind of message is he sending?"

Good times, good times. Good laughs over the crazy frog. Now Mitch would just look at it.

He had absently rubbed away patches of felt and now he could see grim brown plastic showing through on the frog's bulging eye, brown plastic on his crooked little hand. Poor frog looked like a burn victim or something. The frog—both the physical frog and his conflicting semiotics—had attained a vague, mesmerizing pathos.

Jenny tried lots of things to break the spell. She appealed to Mitch's love of their daughter, Becka. She encouraged Mitch to tell his folks he had been laid off. Mitch contended that the shock might be too much for his elderly parents. Jenny suggested that it wasn't healthy to stay in the attic watching a TV with no picture, just sound, and rubbing the felt off his lonesome frog. Mitch said it was the Fox News Channel, you didn't need a picture for that. He said he was up there thinking about the improvements they would make to the attic when he was back on his feet. He said he was drawing up plans in his head. He said boy would Jenny be surprised. He said there was nothing wrong with a man having a little sanctuary in his own home. He said shut the door on your way out.

Finally Jenny invited Mitch's parents over for dinner with explicit instructions for Mitch: By the end of the night he was to tell them the truth. She thought that might help him open up a valve that was closed off. After dinner they put Becka to bed and the grown-ups retired to the living room and sat around looking at one another.

"Well, what now?" said Jenny. It had heft.

"We could have a highball," said Mitch's father.

"We could watch TV," said Mitch.

Jenny gave him that look.

She said, "Well for goodness sakes, Mitch. Your mother and father don't want to watch TV."

"I think it sounds like fun," said Mitch's mother. "We used to watch TV together when Mitch was a little boy. He loved TV so much. I used to say back then that he'd have a job in TV one day. But you're a big responsible man in frozen foods and that's just as exciting in its own way, isn't it?"

"It's not just frozen foods, Mom. It's many kinds of perishable goods. And freezing is hardly the only way of dealing with them."

"Well the important thing is that you have a job, however cockamamie it might be," said Mitch's father.

"Isn't there something you want to tell your parents?" said Jenny.

"I love you, Mom and Dad," said Mitch.

"Well isn't that sweet?" said Mitch's mother. "Just like when he was a little boy."

Jenny left the room.

"My God son, do they let you into work looking like that?" said Mitch's father.

"Sure they do, Dad. It's not like the old days."

"Yes, God forbid a man should take pride in his personal appearance. We're much too sophisticated for that now. I must admit that if looking like a bum is the new measure of a man, you take the cake, son. You truly take the cake. Congratulations. I crown thee king of the bums."

"It's just not like the old days."

"When dinosaurs roamed the earth! Well, you should at least get rid of that stubble. You look like the proverbial Okie from Muskogee. And my God, son, there's a kind of a Z in your hair that's turned white. When did that happen, overnight?"

"My hair is white but not with years, nor grew it white in a single night as men's has grown from sudden fears," said Mitch's mother.

"What in the hell are you babbling about?" said Mitch's father.

"Lord Byron. Oh, I know! We could watch that *Soprano* show I've heard so much about."

"*The Sopranos*?" said Mitch.

"Yes! *The New York Times* calls it worthy of Balzac."

"I don't know, Mom. It's kind of rough."

"You know son, there are commercial dyes for problems such as yours," said Mitch's father. "Not to mention a wonderful invention called the razor. You have a Z in your hair and a V on your forehead. All the last and least worthy letters of the alphabet."

It was true that Mitch had a V-shaped splotch on his forehead, barely discernable most of the time but brightening to red when he became distressed. He could feel it beginning to glow.

"I'd hate to find out where the X and Y are," said Mitch's father. "Not a pretty sight, I'm sure."

"Arthur Dimmesdale was discovered to sport a scarlet A on his very chest," said Mitch's mother. "Whether a natural occurrence due to stress or a self-inflicted mortification of the flesh, I don't believe Hawthorne makes it clear."

"Yes, we are all painfully aware of your lofty educational background, blabbermouth," said Mitch's father. "I was always too busy keeping the family alive to go prancing around a pasture with a volume of poesy."

"I love Balzac," said Mitch's mother. "Isn't that funny. I don't know why Lord Byron reminded me of Balzac. And Balzac reminded me of the *Soprano* show! It certainly is a funny world."

"Not often does a series come along that deserves to be called a masterpiece, but we say, 'Hats off to *The Sopranos*!'" said Mitch's father.

"Who said that?"

"That's my own, son. I just made it up. Your parents are not idiots, I'm sorry to inform you. I know you'd relish the chance to believe otherwise. Life would be so much simpler then, wouldn't it? Only it wouldn't."

Jenny came in with a highball for Mitch's father.

"Oh, well thank you, dear."

"Dad and Mom want to watch *The Sopranos*," Mitch said.

"*The Sopranos* is worthy of Balzac," said Mitch's mother.

"You don't say. Well, I have some calls to make for work. You guys enjoy. Or you know what? You and your parents could talk."

Jenny left.

"I don't know—" said Mitch. "They've been in reruns for an eternity."

"What, are you worried about my delicate sensibilities? Hell, boy, your mother and I have been around the block a few times as they say. We went to see *The Godfather* when it was first in the theaters. Though such an attack of culture on the part of your doddering progenitors comes as a shock to you, no doubt."

"I wasn't crazy about the language, but that Al Pacino is so *cute*," said Mitch's mother. "I like that Gene Wilder, too."

"Gene Wilder wasn't in *The Godfather*," said Mitch's father.

"I *know*, dear. I just think he's cute."

"Well, you know," said Mitch, "*The Sopranos* is pretty complex and involved, I mean there's four or five year's worth of story lines to get familiar with. I'm not sure it would be much fun to watch, you know, just a random rerun of it. But we could watch something else. We don't have to *talk*."

"You're right son," said Mitch's father. "Two drooling mongoloids such as your parents could never figure out something as sophisticated and wonderful as a television program. You had best put it on the mongoloid channel, the special channel that caters to mongoloids."

Mitch's father took a swig of his drink and relaxed his mouth to let some dribble out, to reflect, apparently, his idea of the way Mitch saw him.

"You win," said Mitch.

"No, we're too stupid," said Mitch's father. "Two people as stupid and feeble as your mother and I couldn't possibly win against the likes of you, a man with a Z in his hair."

But yes, he had won.

The Sopranos began in the strip club owned by Tony Soprano, the main character.

"Dear me," said Mitch's mother.

"Oh God," said Mitch, and reached for the remote.

"No dear, it's fine. It's just the *milieu*. They're establishing the *milieu*, just like Balzac would do."

Then came a part about Meadow, Tony Soprano's daughter, who was having trouble with her boyfriend and her college roommate. Mitch's mother brightened.

"Oh! There were daughters in *Père Goriot*!" she said.

Most of the episode was about a sweet-natured pregnant young stripper. Someone smashed her head against the hood of a car. Mitch flipped to the next channel.

"For God's sake, we're not children," said Mitch's father, who was next to him on the sofa.

"Balzac never shied from the less pleasant side of life. Look at *La Comedie humaine*," said Mitch's mother. Mitch watched her, a flickering silhouette in the easy chair, her glasses two TV screens. Mitch's father grabbed the remote and put it back on *The Sopranos*.

"No, I really want to see this television masterpiece of yours," he said.

"Of mine?" said Mitch.

A character expressed his wish to make the pretty young stripper cry; he seemed to accomplish this by forcing her into an unusual and humiliating sexual situation with himself and a policeman. Then the character beat the sweet young stripper with his fists and beat her and beat her until the blood poured out of her face and head and then he beat her some more though she was helpless and limp and he kept on beating her and finally he slammed her head against a railing and gore besmeared it and she was dead. The end.

Mitch's father turned off the television and stood up.

"Thank you for a wonderful evening," he said.

After they left Mitch went out and started raking in the middle of the night.

Jenny stood in the doorway and asked him what he was doing.

"What does it look like I'm doing? Raking. You ought to be happy. You keep telling me to get active."

"Come in, honey. You're going to wake up Becka."

"*You're* going to wake up Becka with all your talking. Raking is a very quiet activity except for the pleasant sound of the rake raking up leaves."

He demonstrated.

Jenny watched for a minute then went inside and shut the door. After awhile all the lights in the house went off. Mitch kept raking.

He saw his crazy neighbors watching him through their blinds.

"That's right, get a good look," he said. He kept raking. "I'm raking at night. That's pretty crazy, all right. That's just about as crazy as the time you painted your latticework at one A.M. Painted it all except for one four foot circular area. That's right, people notice things like that. And I might mention you *still* haven't painted your little four foot circular area, and that was a year and a half ago. That's right, I'm talking to you."

He kept raking.

"I couldn't even see your damn latticework if you hadn't cut down that tree," he said, pretty much to himself. "The one thing that afforded us any privacy from each other. Cut it down for no reason! It wasn't bothering anybody. And then it just lay there in your yard like a corpse for four months."

Mitch stopped raking. He couldn't see the crazy neighbors anymore, but he hoped they were still watching. He hoped they were watching because he stopped, put his hand on his hip, and stared at the blue tarp on top of their house.

That's right, I'm looking at your tarp, he thought. You want to watch me rake leaves? Well, guess what. I want to look at your stupid tarp. Damaged shingles. Those shingles sure have been damaged for a long time. Three years. Three years of damaged shingles. The guy drives to work every day in a pick-up with a huge trailer on it. Among the items in the trailer: stacks and stacks and stacks of brand new shingles. That's right.

"Mitch, are you going to stay out there all night?"

It was Jenny again.

"What's it to you?"

"Mitch."

"Were you watching me?" Mitch said. "Did you get a good look?"

"Yes, I was watching you stare at the sky for ten minutes, if that's what you mean."

"I was not staring at the sky. I was staring at *their damn tarp*!" Mitch deliberately shouted the last three words in the direction of the crazy neighbors' house.

"Mitch! Hush up now and come inside."

"Damaged shingles," Mitch said.

Jenny awoke that night to find Mitch standing by the bedroom window, curtain parted, peeking out.

"Mitch?"

"You're not going to believe this."

"Mitch?"

"They're weeding."

"What?"

"The crazy neighbors are out there pulling weeds at three A.M. With a flashlight. I mean, he's holding a flashlight and she's pulling weeds."

"Oh well," said Jenny.

"Are they trying to make a comment? I mean, is that a gesture pointed in my direction?"

"I doubt it," said Jenny.

"A gesture of defiance?"

"I don't think so."

"Like, 'You think you're so great raking. Well, look at us, we can pull weeds.'"

"I don't know, maybe you inspired them."

"Inspired them to mock me."

"Come to bed, honey."

"But that would imply they know I'm watching."

Jenny made a noise and rolled over.

Mitch shivered violently.

"They *know I'm watching*," he said in a hoarse whisper.

"Mitch, honey, I have to be at work early tomorrow."

"Oh! Meaning you have a job and I don't."

"Mitch…"

"Very subtle."

He came to bed.

"I know one thing for sure," he said.

He waited for Jenny to say, "What's that?" She didn't. He answered anyway:

"From now on I'm going to rake in the daylight, like a normal person."

He waited for Jenny to tell him he *was* a normal person, he was just under a lot of stress, that's all.

He waited.

"They've held a mirror up to my madness, that's what they've done. I'll be damned if I let them drag me down to their level," he said.

"Mm," Jenny said.

"In a way I should thank them."

After awhile Jenny's breath steadied into the soft lulled lapping of sleep.

"Hey," Mitch said loudly.

Jenny stirred but didn't quite seem to wake.

"Yep," Mitch said. "Yep, yep."

He waited a minute.

"Yep! Yep!"

She was asleep all right.

Mitch got up and opened and shut some drawers.

"Honey, what are you doing?"

"They have a traditional thirties style bungalow," Mitch said.

"I know, honey."

"And yet they have doors..."

"From a Chinese restaurant, I know."

"Ornately carved bright red doors!"

"You're not telling me anything I don't know."

"Huge doors! Palatial! As if from a Chinese restaurant! And there are no knobs on the doors."

"Mitch..."

"You have to *stick your hand in the hole* to open the doors! Big gaping holes where the knobs should be!"

"Come to bed."

"The doors to their house! The front doors! Doors without knobs!"

"Mitch, do you think you ought to talk to somebody?"

"About what?"

The next day began Mitch's raking period, as well as his disregard of, casual amusement about, growing fascination with, comforting by, sneaky dread of, unpleasant feelings around, glum resignation to, eventual disillusionment with and cold disgust over the punctuality of the squirrels. Jenny knew something was wrong because he made hardly any mention of the neighbors' erection of a chunky, imposing black iron fence *or* their purchase of a loud, ugly dog. Nor did he make a fuss on the morning they discovered that the fence's tumescent black pineapple-shaped finials had been painted sloppy gold in the middle of the night.

On the Saturday before Becka's fourth birthday, she had a play date with a couple of kids from daycare. The mommies drank a little white wine while the kids waddled around with fistfuls of cupcake and had a good time. There were a lot of bumping noises coming from the attic. One of the women finally mentioned it.

"Oh you know men with their projects," Jenny said.

The other women shifted, uneasy. Everyone knew that Mitch had been laid off. So what? It wasn't a crime. Still, you would think that Jenny had referred not to her husband, but to something slight and distasteful, like a fart.

The bumping noises went on but no one mentioned them again. Jenny wondered if something sinister and depressive might be taking hold in the attic. No, no, Mitch just didn't want to mingle, that's all, he never had, even before the layoff. The attic was, at this specific moment, better than raking, wasn't it? In the attic he was sequestered, not openly yelling at a squirrel that refused to budge from a knot—*losing* an argument with a squirrel.

After the women and children had gone, Jenny heard the attic door open.

"Are the crones gone?" Mitch called down.

"Yes," said Jenny. "I mean, they're hardly crones. Most of them are about half our age, I would say."

"Oh. What does crone mean?"

"I think it refers to an old hag."

"Oh, I thought it meant crow. Like a magpie or crow. Like a bird that just yaps all the time."

"I don't like yelling up at you when I can't see you," said Jenny.

"It's all right, I'm coming down."

When Mitch appeared he was holding a long, rectangular box wrapped in flowery paper.

"Where's Becka?" he said.

Jenny smiled and pointed. Becka was conked out, her cheek flat on the cool foyer floor. "I was just about to put her in bed."

"Aw, come on, wake her up, I got her a present."

"What is it?"

"It's not *your* present. You'll see when she opens it."

"Well, her birthday's not until Monday. Can't she open it then?"

"Come on, butterball," Mitch said to Becka. He propped her against the wall. "Don't you want to see what Daddy got you? Go ahead and open it, big ol' butterball."

Becka looked kind of woozy.

"Too much candy and cake, huh? That's my girl! Here, Daddy'll help."

Jenny stood and watched as Mitch squatted on the floor and unwrapped the box.

"You know what you do with that, sweetness? You can look at the moon with it, that's what."

"You bought our daughter a telescope. For her fourth birthday."

"Aw, come on, Jenny, it's a birdwatching telescope is all it is. It's not like what they have at the Griffith Observatory or anything. It's not an electron microscope or anything. It's something so she can enjoy the wonders of nature."

"Looks like she's raring to go," Jenny said.

Becka had fallen asleep against the wall.

"Now that's not fair. I think she'll get a kick out of it."

"Well, I just don't think she's quite ready for a telescope," Jenny said.

Mitch was busy taking the telescope out of the box. It was a plain white tube with black trim.

"What?" he said.

"I'm not sure it's age appropriate. It's bigger than she is."

"Right, right." He was putting it together.

"Uhm, what are you doing?"

"Huh?"

"Are you putting that telescope together?"

"I thought I might try it out."

"On what?" Jenny said slowly.

"Well, now that you mention it..."

"Oh, I knew it," Jenny said.

She swooped down and picked up Becka, headed with her toward the bedroom. Mitch followed, the partially assembled telescope in hand.

"What did you know?" he said. "What did you know?"

"Shh," said Jenny.

"What did you know? I just want to know what you know. What you think you know."

"I don't know."

"What? Do you think I'm going to do something *weird* with this telescope?"

Jenny was taking off Becka's shoes and socks.

"I just thought I'd observe the squirrels, you know, from a distance. I mean, don't you think it's strange at all that they *only* come out when I'm raking, and they *only* sit in their chosen spots?"

"It's strange all right," said Jenny.

She tucked Becka in.

"Well, what is this gravitation they feel toward me? It creeps me out to tell you the truth. What am I, the mothership? The mothership connection?"

"I don't know."

"Remember that? Parliament Funkadelic? *The Mothership Connection*? Bootsy Collins?"

"Bootsy Collins is not my main concern at the moment."

"Aw, come on. Lighten up. I'm going to make some observations, that's all. I think these squirrels are exhibiting some pretty strange behavior. I just want to know if they sit in that hollow and on that knot when I'm not around. Because it's pretty clear they're interested in me. I'm not saying that in a paranoid way. I'm sure it's just a phenomenon of nature gone awry, you know, like when baby ducks start following around a cat or something."

"When baby ducks follow a *cat*?"

"It was on the news once. You saw it. The orphaned baby ducks that mistook a cat for their mother? Anyway, that's not the point. It's like that old thing, does the refrigerator light really go off when you shut the door? Or like when you were a kid and you wondered if your stuffed animals came to life when you left the room."

"I never thought that."

"Well, I can't help it if you were an unimaginative child."

Mitch followed Jenny out of the room.

He said, "All I want to do I just want to take some notes, record some data. Maybe I'm onto something."

He touched her shoulder. They stopped, face to face, at the bottom of the attic stairs.

"Jenny, this is important to me. It's not just about squirrels. I've been having trouble finding a job, you know."

"I know, honey," she said tenderly.

"So I've been thinking, and I finally decided I want to take a shot at becoming a naturalist."

Jenny smiled. Her eyes got big. She laughed joyfully, as if expecting Mitch to do the same.

"What," he said.

"You're going to become a naturalist," she said with a big, friendly smile.

"I'm seriously considering it, yes."

"The man who doesn't know the difference between a crow and a crone."

She laughed a little, kindly. Mitch didn't laugh.

"People become naturalists," he said. "It's something people do. Face it. Face reality. People become naturalists every day. Every naturalist there is, well, at some point he had to say, the hell with it, to hell with the strictures of this workaday world, I'm going to become a naturalist, right? Right? There has to be a conscious decision, right? I don't mock your dreams."

"Okay, honey," said Jenny.

"I wish you wouldn't look all—" He couldn't think of the word. "This is not unprecedented. It's not a bolt from the blue. There was some accuracy, some skill, some *science* involved with my former profession, I know it pains you to realize it. Supply chain dynamics and strategies are not the province of imbeciles and dolts, I'm sorry to be the first to break it to you."

"When did your father walk into the house? Because you sound exactly like your father."

"Now you're just trying to be hurtful. Listen. Remember how I told you when I was in college and I used to skip class and watch the ducks on the frozen pond? You remember. Some of the ducks would jump up and down and loosen the ice in the middle of the pond?"

Jenny shook her head.

"You remember, all right. Once there was enough water exposed, one group of ducks would hop in and swim in circles, widening the circumference of the liquid part of the pond. And at the same time, you know, another group of ducks would stand around them and continue to jump up and down to loosen the ice. It was teamwork. They actually worked in shifts. It was cooperation within the animal kingdom."

"That's a great story," Jenny said.

"Well, I found it fascinating. If you can't understand that, I feel sorry for you, frankly."

He started up the stairs with his telescope.

"So it's back to the attic now," Jenny said with a sickly kind of resigned, frustrated, tightlipped humor.

"Yes, it's back to the attic now," said Mitch.

"Where you're going to relive some of the adventures of your youth."

He turned and looked at her from the top of the stairs. He didn't answer, but his V was enflamed.

"Gorillas in the mist. Watching the ducks on the frozen pond," Jenny said.

Mitch went inside and shut the attic door.

It wasn't long afterward that someone rang the bell. Jenny saw one of the crazy neighbors through the beveled glass.

She opened the door a crack.

"Hi," she said.

"Tell your husband to stop watching us through a telescope."

"I was looking at my squirrel!" Mitch yelled down.

"Yeah well you tell him he can go to jail for looking at squirrels," said the crazy neighbor.

Winter came.

The squirrels moved on.

Mitch watched the blackbirds in the crazy neighbors' yard but it wasn't the same. He put down the telescope and pressed his forehead against the cold window. He counted at least twenty blackbirds, their wings purple and black, their eyes yellow and green, stony eyes, as he knew from his long periods of observation.

None of the mirth of squirrels.

The humorless blackbirds stole the dog's food, choked the pellets down their skinny beaks, they fought for the food now and then, they hopped cruel and mechanical on the dry December grass.

Mitch rapped at the window, pretty softly, and the blackbirds shot away. How do they hear something so soft? How do they know it is directed at them out of all the sounds in the world? What is the difference between blackbirds and crows, if any?

Nature was full of mysteries, waiting for someone like Mitch to unlock them.

The birds settled and resettled in the yard, only to be shooed away for good by the bang of a tailgate. Mitch was surprised to see a moving van parked crookedly in front of the crazy neighbors' house, half on the sidewalk. Pretty soon he saw the crazy neighbors come out of the house and drop an upright piano. The top came open like a sleeping drunk's mouth. The crazy neighbors stood there cussing at the piano like they expected it to get up and walk into the truck on its own. For some reason it gave Mitch no pleasure.

He picked up the telescope and surveyed the situation. He reviewed the brown leaves and black branches nesting in the whorls and eddies of the parched and livid tarp, until a couple of guys in blue uniforms came up a ladder and removed it. The shingles that had been hidden beneath the tarp were perfect.

Mitch focused the telescope. Put it down. Returned it to his eye. Beheld the perfect shingles. Put the telescope down. Rested his head against the window.

Perfect.

The crazy neighbors sped away with all their belongings and a nice new family moved in right behind them, a family who fixed the latticework and repainted the pineapples a proper black—no, of course not, of course they went ahead and knocked down the fence. Mitch saw the kids move out and the nice young couple grow old and die, he saw a series of houses being built and razed on the same spot and flowers blooming and crumpling, blooming and crumpling, right before his eyes, and clouds and traffic sweeping by, the sun bouncing up and down and up and down, a skyscraper rising in the neighbors' yard, imploded almost immediately by a tiny, scurrying demolition crew, and another tower rising and falling, another, and finally some kind of crazy future building made of glass and chrome, decorated with Saturn-like rings, and citizens of the universe flying by in small personal helicopters, until the tower of the future was strangled by ivy, and lava covered the face of the land. And Mitch stood still the whole time while the world blossomed and died around him, with his head pressed to the cold glass just like that.

MY HIGH, SQUEAKY VOICE

People love my high, squeaky voice. What's not to love? It's high and it's squeaky. And it is mine. I love the way God made me.

I have made a wonderful tape of me speaking normally. Normally for me is a high, squeaky voice. I have sent out my tape to many companies that produce audio books. I think people would like to drive around in their cars listening to me read mystery stories in my high, squeaky voice.

Friends have told me that they could listen to my high, squeaky voice all day long. When I say something they say, say that again. They love to hear me talk in my high, squeaky voice.

I have received many letters from the producers of audio books. I keep the letters in a drawer for evidence. The letters seem to be printed by a machine with no human contact. They seem to be almost exactly the same even though they come from different companies. Different cities and towns. I think that is an odd coincidence. They regret they have to return my tapes. I do not suit their needs at the present time. They do not accept unsolicited materials. Etc. It is very odd that all the letters say the same thing. I am keeping them in a drawer for evidence. I suppose it is not fashionable to have a high, squeaky voice. I say, precisely. Fashionable means nothing to me. If you choose to disregard me based on my high, squeaky voice there is a word for that. That word is called censorship. And it is wrong. For man looks on the outward appearance but the Lord looketh upon the heart. What a person looks like on the outside does not matter. What a person looks like on the inside is what matters. God does not make trash. Anyway, who is riding around in their car thinking I like this audio book but I wonder if this man has one arm or two? I wonder what he weighs? All they really care about is if they like your high, squeaky voice. If I just had a chance.

Friends have told me to follow your dreams. You can do anything you set your mind to. One day I know I will be a reader for a company that produces audio books. I like mystery stories the best but I will read anything they want me to. Friends have joked they would listen to me read a phone book with my high, squeaky voice. One thing I will not read is erotica.

Another one is writings against Christ.

I went to the library and got on the computer. You would not believe what happened when I typed in audio books. I almost started to cry. How would I ever look at so many things about audio books? They would shut down the library before I got halfway done. Maybe I could hide in the bathroom until everyone had gone home and then continue to look at the computer. If I started to cry too loud they would put me out then and there. I have had run-ins with the library guards. They are rough men.

It is no use being a downer. If God is for us who can be against us? Focus on the positive and not the negative. At least I have a computer. At least I have found these writings about audio books.

I admired the standards of the audio book companies. This one said we only produce work of the highest caliber.

Check.

Another one said the finest recording techniques.

Check.

Another one said popular titles read by world-class talent.

Check.

Not once did someone say we do not like somebody with a high, squeaky voice.

What is the matter with me? I obey all their rules. Sometimes I feel like it does not matter. It would not matter if I was a famous athlete or a king. No matter what I was they would never accept me. I would never have my dream. That is called censorship. And it is wrong. I don't care if the whole world is wrong if I know I am right. And I know I am right even if the whole world is wrong. If God is for us who can be against us?

Yes I know library patrons are not allowed behind that library counter. That library counter is for library workers only. Yes I have been told many times. But Miss Violet is my friend. She likes my high, squeaky voice. Everything is not just official between me and Miss Violet. Sometimes everything cannot be official. Sometimes everything cannot follow the rules. Sometimes rules are made to be broken. A friend in need is a friend indeed. George Bush's father signed the bill into law. It is called the Americans with Disabilities Act. This is not erotica. I just needed to talk. I just needed a shoulder to lean on. I needed a shoulder to cry on. I needed to see a friendly face. I needed a friendly hello. Sometimes you want to go where everybody knows your name. Sometimes I get distracted when I am thinking about other things.

I respect that people become upset. This is what society has taught us. Always put your clothes on or you are a bad person. With so many problems in the world why do we care if I put my clothes on? Why do you care so much about the way God made me? Are you mad at God?

That is your problem not mine.

THE MYSTERIOUS SECRET OF THE VALUABLE TREASURE

Introduction

The death records of Boyle County are numerous and varied. The yellow fever epidemic. A man crushed by stones. A refrigerator fell on a baby.

Modern historians are fascinated by such tales of woe. But what of our ancestors in their happier moments? Lemonade was just the thing on a hot day! Let's have a taffy pull after Sunday school was a sentiment often to be heard.

If it is a crime to dwell upon the lighter side of life then lock me up! Those seeking gloom and doom are advised to look elsewhere. For those of a gentler nature I trust that they will find many treats and surprises nestled within, like walnuts and oranges bursting forth from the innards of a gaily striped sock upon some faraway Christmas morn.

I can already hear the scandalized objections of some wags who proclaim: could this really be Willie Dobbs attempting to pen a history of our fair community? The laziest man in town!

Such criticisms are all too true. And yet without my personal problems I would have never found the time nor the inclination to write a history of South Preston.

In fabled times of days of yore, only the "landed gentry" had time to write and contemplate. In today's modern age, it is the unemployed and the upset who enjoy such luxuries. For example, had I never lost my job I would have never discovered my favorite barbecue restaurant.

It was within the walls of the historic graveyard next to that very same restaurant where I first discovered my fondness for rubbing. On many a day after a satisfying meal of barbecue I could be found clasping a sturdy piece of paper to the face of a historic gravestone and rubbing most enthusiastically with a large flat charcoal pencil designed expressly for the purpose, thereby producing a "copy" of said gravestone for later enjoyment.

From those noble environs it was a short step, mentally, to the courthouse and the local library. Where else but in the musty corridors of the humble library may one find examples of old newspaper advertisements?

Even before I realized that my avocation might bear creative fruit I spent several golden afternoons amusing myself with such unlikely products as spats, unguents and girdles. Slowly the forces of inspiration dawned upon me. If Willie Dobbs could find enjoyment through this simple trip down "memory lane" why not the residents of South Preston at large? In business parlance, I had discovered my "market." Little did I know that my life would be transformed in a nonce from one of scholarly concerns into a thrill-a-minute tangle of passion and suspense. And murder!!!

How did I, an aspiring amateur historian of South Preston, wind up seeking ill-gotten riches in the lawless "mean streets" of neighboring Newberry? The story is an extremely tedious one. Around Chapter Five, however, the action picks up considerably. Then it dies down again for a few chapters. But after that it is nothing but action all the way to the end.

Hereby I hope that I have prickled the natural curiosity of you, the human reader! And yet if a single schoolchild merely approaches the vicinity of the library in search of more information, I feel that I will have done my job.

Chapter One
Look Out! The Indians of South Preston

Many wags have noted that there is not a North Preston. So why do we call ourselves South Preston? This is a favorite joke of some wags. But to understand the history of South Preston we need to be serious for a moment. Before South Preston was called South Preston it was called something else by the Indians who lived here. These were a fierce people who enjoyed activities such as raping and cannibalizing.

Elaborate masks were worn at certain ceremonies.

The Indians had a relationship to the land.

Eventually their population died out due to diseases.

On boyhood field trips to Fort Martin a search for arrowheads was a favorite activity! No arrowheads were usually found. But that did not stop an optimistic ten-year-old from looking! More often than not the boys in question did not heed the informative lectures of the Fort Martin tour guide, who was always dressed in a sparkling costume of authenticity. We have plenty of time for lectures later! was our boyish thought. If we could just find one arrowhead we believed that our fortunes would be made. The actual cannon on the premises was also enjoyable for looking and touching. This cannon was last restored in 1979 by the South Preston Jaycees.

Alas the only visible arrowheads were located within the Fort Martin Gift Shop. These arrowheads were considered too expensive by the parents of the day, which was around 1973.

It was on one such lark that I was tricked into putting dog poop into my mouth by Scott Turner. The circumstances were this: Scott had gone to some great length to fashion a piece of dog poop into looking like an arrowhead. Everyone knew I was looking for arrowheads.

At the time I chanced upon said "arrowhead," I recall that Scott Turner was standing off to the side with some of his usual "gang," who were snickering and making faces. This would have probably included Jem Vinings, Jed Humphries and one or both of the Rex twins. I am not casting aspersions upon Jed Humphries, whose head was later completely removed from his body in a disaster.

I exclaimed to Scott and his friends that I had found an arrowhead.

Scott informed me very seriously that there was only one surefire way of detecting the authenticity of an arrowhead. He explained that there was a metallic or magnetic component in a genuine arrowhead that would cause a slight, harmless shock if placed in one's mouth.

It was at this juncture that I placed the dog poop in my mouth.

I believe that it was this same field trip whereon I was mocked and jeered at for wearing my grandfather's shoes.

Chapter Two

A Great Itch: The Founding of South Preston

Boyle County was created by a board of commissioners in 1850 by mushing together the unwanted lower portions of two other counties. The happy result was named for Johannes Hubbard Boyle, a respected railroad executive who was literally torn limb from limb.

Cog Creek has been heralded as the central body of water for Boyle County. Today it exists as a dry creek bed. In the halcyon days before a bridge was dreamed of, one relied on a ferry to "tote" one across Cog Creek. Such a device was most often operated by what was called a "darkey" in the usual language of the day. Today we realize that such language is not often appreciated.

Cog Creek first dried up in 1918 and it has never been the same since. The bridge was unnecessarily constructed over dry land in 1922, to the exacerbation of an enraged populace. This led to the famous "Bridge Riots" in which the homes of several local "Negroes" were destroyed.

Coming over the Cog Creek Bridge from an easterly direction by way of neighboring Sproatsborough one first notices the gentle rolling slopes of South Preston. One's eye is next drawn to the old yellow mattresses and filthy plastic diapers that the area's poor continue to throw off the bridge despite numerous ordinances to the contrary. When the accretions of garbage under the Cog Creek Bridge reach a sufficient level, South Preston is visited by flocks of birds that local birdwatchers remain unable to identify. These are known locally as "trash birds" and reach an estimated four feet in height. Their coloring is unattractive and their calls have been compared to the piercing shriek of a cougar or mountain lion. Incidents have been recorded of "trash birds" flying into the open windows of vehicles and biting passengers or drivers in the throat. Those who have been close to them remark on their smell, which is said to be unforgettable.

The first records of the area now known as South Preston date from 1540, when a Spaniard reports receiving a "great itch" nearby. Whether his comment refers to an allergic reaction to local fauna or the contraction of a Native American venereal disease akin to our present-day "crabs," modern historians have not been able to fathom.

Chapter Three
The Great Panic

In 1873 the "Great Panic" swept over the United States, causing people to panic. The citizenry of South Preston was no exception.

The causes of the Great Panic were monetary and economic. There is no good time for a Great Panic! But in the case of South Preston, it could not have come at a worse time, just when the city was running out of decorative rocks.

It was soon discovered that rocks are not a renewable resource such as trees or food. You cannot plant rocks! This fact seems simple to us in our modern world, but it had a devastating effect upon the economy of South Preston. Once-proud mansions, gutted and forlorn, shells of which still dot downtown Front Street, gave solemn, silent testimony to the record number of suicides that occurred in those heady times.

It is all too easy to condemn the suicides of our forefathers thanks to our modern hindsight. Hindsight, it has been claimed with some assurance, is always twenty-twenty! Due to the strict moral codes of Victorian times, however, many of our male ancestors preferred a self-inflicted death over the prospect of one's wife taking on the controversial role known as "breadwinner."

Even in our modern times, vestiges of this discredited attitude continue to haunt South Preston! When I was laid off from my employment nearly five years ago, my wife's parents were openly dismayed that I did not seek new employment right away. My wife also participated in these conversations. The fact that suffrage had long been official United States policy, rendering traditional gender roles forever altered, did not seem to occur to them! It was during one of these "pep talks" from my father-in-law that I first conceived of becoming a historian.

My ambitions at the time were somewhat grander than the limited scope of the present work. Indeed I recall the stunned surprise afflicting my father-in-law's sputtering brow when, upon his query as to whether I intended to remain in the guise of a bum for the rest of my life, I retorted that I was as a matter of fact most assiduously employed—in the writing of a History of the United States!

Though my remark had been the result of a thoughtless blurting, the likelihood of my own words soon began to amaze me. Why, after all, should a "common man" be excluded from the chance to engage himself with so lofty a subject? Would it not be, after all, quintessentially AMERICAN to avail oneself of such attainments? Gumption still counts for something in this country! And I admit that I relished the thought of my erstwhile co-workers marveling thusly: Did you see Willie Dobbs on C-Span last night? He has written an entire History of the United States of America! I am sorry for those things I did to him. Now it is I who look like the fool!

Such dreams, vain though they be, fueled my desire to succeed.

Looking back it is easy to trace the circumstances leading up to my surprising blurt.

To begin with, I had been "making good" on a resolution of self-improvement. I had decided, in short, to use the extra free time vouchsafed for me by my changed situation to "catch up on my reading."

And catch up I did! Beginning with a book called *The French Revolution* by Thomas Carlyle. Carlyle wrote at a time period when language was not as understandable as it is today. Nonetheless I was inspired by his verbal pyrotechnics. As I skimmed his voluble meanderings I could not help but notice that Thomas Carlyle took a casual and personal approach to history. He wrote of great kings of royal blood with the same light familiarity as one might apply to one's "poker buddies" and their tales of friendly roughhousing on an all-male camping trip.

No explanation or precedent, however, could prevent my wife and her immediate family from ridiculing my dreams. Even her brother with whom we have minimal contact felt obliged to call long distance and recite a list of his various displeasures with my life.

I began to lack interest in cleanliness.

I slept very little and ate with the same regrettable negligence.

All this time I roamed the streets of South Preston by night, my head filled with nervous ideas about the wondrous things sure to spurt forth from my pen. It was as if the entire book was already laid out in my head! I could feel its heft and even see the cover, which was festooned with an American flag in the traditional patriotic hues of red, white, and my personal favorite, blue. The sentences whirled in my brain vehemently. Yet they stubbornly refused to submit to the printed page. Indeed I began to notice with a degree of irrational suspicion that each time I was truly ready to begin my History of the United States a mysterious stumbling block had beset my path. For example, I would think about plugging in the computer and a lightning storm would come up out of nowhere. Or I would get home and notice that the box of paper I had purchased looked unprofessional.

It was at or around this juncture that I began to have troubling thoughts, such as, what if I am a serial killer without knowing it? Amnesia or psychosis might play a part in my nightly walks! Large portions of which I remembered only as a black space in my brain.

My thoughts along these lines became more elaborate. Such as, what if an excess of earwax is pressing into my brain and causing me to exhibit serial killer behavior? Or even if I am not a serial killer yet, is it only a matter of time? Will the earwax that is pressing into my brain and causing these ruminations eventually accumulate to such an extent that I will be helpless to resist my innate impulses to be a serial killer? At the time I was afflicted with what seemed to be an untoward amount of earwax, my concern with which gave rise to my troubling and groundless thoughts.

The situation was not aided by the incessant jesting of my father-in-law, which was along the lines of How's it going professor? and other demeaning comments. The fact that circumstances had prevented me from producing a single word of my intended opus only added fodder to these hurtful jests. It was like a self-fulfilling prophecy come true!

The normally sanguine holiday of Thanksgiving proved especially distressing. It was our turn to host the festivities, and you may be sure that all those present concentrated the full force of their discernment upon detecting some hint of our depleted circumstances in the meal with which we presented them—and which, by the bye, they managed to stuff quite handily into their ravening craws. Sad, knowing looks were exchanged all about the table as our apparently shameful cranberry sauce slumped upon its plate, telltale indentations revealing its provenance as a lowly can.

I only use fresh cranberries sighed one mournful consumer.

That's funny I retorted. There is no such thing as fresh cranberries in South Preston!

These days you can get anything fresh the mopey harridan insisted.

Naturally almost everyone jumped in to take her side including my own wife.

Anything fresh. How can you get anything fresh I demanded.

The internet was her laughable assertion.

I am a man who spent 18 years in supply chain management I rebutted.

What the hell has that got to do with it her cross-eyed husband wished to inquire.

I then explained to one and all assembled, though they already knew it very well, that food transport logistics had been my special area. You can get many things fresh in South Preston but one thing you cannot get fresh in South Preston is cranberries! Trust me!

Frozen is the same as fresh whimpered the mistaken harpy.

At this juncture my increasingly reddened father-in-law maliciously switched the subject to my History of the United States.

I should not have been surprised to discover that everyone was familiar with the ambitious project, and that the mere mention of it drove them into helpless fits of conspiratorial hilarity designed to make me feel bad about myself as a human being.

Do you know how much he spent on this expletive my father-in-law demanded.

People made several guesses as to the amount of "seed money" I had laid out for the furtherance of my creative endeavors. I had, in fact, purchased around two thousand dollars worth of research materials from amazon.com to help me get jumpstarted. A History of the United States does not write itself! Things must be looked up! When my father-in-law "wowed" them with the figure in question, those present playacted as if they had never dreamed of such a magnificent sum. These people who prided themselves upon pragmatism did not agree with the quintessentially American supposition that one must spend money to make money! My father-in-law then chose to lord it over me that he had "loaned" me the money I had spent on my research materials. According to his estimation, I had not used this "loan" for its intended purpose of fixing the large holes in the kitchen, hallway and bedroom floors.

Some things are more important than holes in floors I elucidated calmly.

Tell that to the doctor when somebody breaks their ankle my father-in-law intoned ominously, whereupon—as if coached in advance!—the assemblage proceeded to conceive it as great sport that an individual would spend money in the acquisition of knowledge.

Yes Mr. Big Shot my father-in-law chimed in derisively. I guess you know everything there is to know about America.

I know a thing or two I riposted assuredly.

You don't know expletive my father-in-law snarled animalistically.

It was at this juncture that I stormed from the room understandably.

When I returned, the evidence I had been seeking firmly in hand, it was clear that everyone had been discussing my shortcomings, for a sudden hush fell over the conversation and I was stared upon by numerous eyes full of misguided and hypocritical "sympathy."

Let me show you the kind of thing you are making fun of I uttered.

Yes we would love to hear it came the sneering reply.

This is one of the founding documents of our nation I pronounced. *Of Plymouth Plantation* by William Bradford. This is where we get our modern ideas of Thanksgiving that we are celebrating this very day.

I learned everything I needed to know about Thanksgiving as a two-year-old my father-in-law boasted smugly. The Indians brought over some corn. Everybody had a good time. End of story. America is not about book learning it is about common sense he concluded erroneously.

My attractive young sister-in-law intervened precipitously. I think it would be nice to hear about the first Thanksgiving she cooed warmingly.

With that welcome and all-too-rare modicum of encouragement I opened the tome in question and read aloud at random from Chapter XXXII, "Wickedness Breaks Forth":

There was a youth whose name was Thomas Granger. He was servant to an honest man of Duxbury, being about 16 or 17 years of age… He was this year detected of buggery, and indicted for the same, with a mare, a cow, two goats, five sheep, two calves and a turkey. Horrible it is to mention, but the truth of the history requires it.

Well that tears it my father-in-law interrupted feverishly. That's fine talk for Thanksgiving dinner, some nincompoop screwing a turkey.

Truth be told I shared his incredulity, though I was not in a position to give him any quarter; to do so would have been to admit defeat. It was my first time opening the book and I was as shocked as anyone by its pornographic content. Yet my rage and vulnerability at being treated like a buffoon in my own household overtook my better judgement, and I must admit I enjoyed some pleasure knowing that words of William Bradford—an unimpeachable source on the face of it!—were causing such consternation and even, in the case of my mother-in-law, signs of physical illness and discomfort. Though I knew it was wrong I continued to orate perversely:

And whereas some of the sheep could not so well be known by his description of them, others with them were brought before him and he declared which were they and which were not. And accordingly he was cast by the jury and condemned, and after executed about the 8th of September, 1642. A very sad spectacle it was. For first the mare and then the cow and the rest of the lesser cattle were killed before his face, according to the law, Leviticus xx.15; and then he himself was executed. The cattle were all cast into a great large pit that was digged of purpose for them, and no use made of any part of them.

I found that I was weeping uncontrollably.

I don't see why they had to kill the poor cows my limpid-eyed sister-in-law averred goodheartedly. It wasn't their fault.

Are you kidding me? my father-in-law bellowed, rising startlingly. Get your damn coat Mabel we are out of here!

My mother-in-law required assistance to be removed.

I must admit that I too had become disheartened by the shenanigans of the day. Was this the history of our country? My intended project opened at my feet like a remorseful abscess, like the puckered anus of an innocent lamb crawling with loathsome disease. Why the simplest childish holiday pageant held within it more patriotism and truth than the "accurate" rantings of our smut-obsessed forefathers!

Almost five years passed. It was at this juncture that I gained in excess of sixty pounds. I was no longer the man my wife had married! All I wanted to do was eat barbecue and walk around the graveyard, struck by the reality of death.

Chapter Four
"The Great South Preston Sheep"... and Other Hauntings!

No town worth its salt would be "caught dead" without its chilling tales of "spooks" and "creeps." South Preston is certainly no exception to this delightfully spooky rule!

The "Sheep Man of Cog Creek," South Preston's answer to such popular legends as "Bigfoot" and "Jack the Ripper," was said to be like a large sheep who walked upright on two legs. This unconfirmed creature was blamed for a mysterious rash of items being moved from one place to another in the early part of the twentieth century.

We would probably not recall the "Sheep Man" today if this intriguing figure had not been forever immortalized in the writings of Esther Leland Hope (1893-1978). Miss Hope is remembered by most as an elderly lady who baked cookies. But anyone who was a schoolboy in the latter days of the 1960s will recall having to learn by rote her famous versification on the proud local subject of the "Sheep Man." The memorable final couplet is still as vivid to me as it was the day I stood before Miss McCord's second grade classroom and declaimed:

We hark! thy plaintive bleat;
Tis neither man nor neither beast
But the Great South Preston Sheep!

It was through the work of Miss Hope that I became acquainted with several other local folktales of a supernatural bent.

Esther Leland Hope is somewhat of a local legend herself. Her privately owned publishing concern, The Ambrosia Press, was one of the first examples of female entrepreneurship in South Preston, at a time when such endeavors were looked upon as a sign of mannishness and lesbianism. Miss Hope was a woman of high energies, as attested to by the astonishing number—far too great to list here—of the tracts she produced outlining her controversial stance on the Jewish religion. But her most helpful work, in light of our present concerns, is 1952's *Boyle County Ghosts*. The Ambrosia Press had long ceased business, and *Boyle County Ghosts* was published by the prestigious U-Publish-It company of Terrytown, New York.

How do you know the cemetery is popular? asks one old saw. Because people are "dying to get in" comes the humorous riposte! Conversely, people must be "dying to get out" of South Preston, for the number of spectral presences opting to stay put in local "haunts" is low and paltry according to Miss Hope's research on the subject. But my "pun" is merely a humorous remark and does not reflect upon the multifarious pleasures of the South Preston lifestyle.

Nevertheless South Preston ghosts are by far the minority in *Boyle County Ghosts*, with the greatest accretion of numinous ectoplasm appearing in Bunt and Newberry, which is perhaps to be expected, as the latter is the county seat. Even ghosts hanker after the prestige and gourmet coffee bars of the "big city," it would seem! The larger populations of the forenamed cities would also mathematically produce by logic a larger number of ghosts, just as there is a larger number of Hispanics in Newberry, or conjoined twins.

Ghosts do not, of course, exist, so perhaps the point is moot. In any case, what South Preston "ghouls" lack in quantity, they make up for in extra spookiness! Here, as corroboration, I present Miss Hope's findings on the subject, changing just enough words, from my small understanding of the law, to avoid any prosecution on charges of plagiarism:

It is said that in the nineteenth century a certain gentleman of the town enjoyed throwing Christian children down a well based on the false assumption that it would make his crops grow. He was brought to justice by an unruly mob. It is said that the cries of the Christian children continue to call for his blood from the depths of the mysterious well of this unrepentantly child-killing fellow.

Another creepy tale recounts the courtship of a young South Preston couple at the turn of the century. On the day they were scheduled to marry, a sultry, raven-locked "Jewess" (Miss Hope's own colorful term!), her advances having been rejected by the groom on religious and moral grounds, sliced off the unfortunate bride's head with a scythe she had brought along for the purpose, as the lovely bride knelt by her bed unawares, asking the Savior's blessing upon her nuptial day. The headless bride is said to stalk the halls of her ancestral home, piteously weeping, presumably from her neck-hole or some other handy orifice.

At this juncture it behooves me to pen a few words in defense of

Judaism.

The Jewish people have been known to contribute many items of salutary effect to humanity as a whole, such as the polio vaccine. Albert Einstein, thought by many to be one of the smartest persons in history, was Jewish. Though you may not know it, many of your favorite comedians who bring such amusement and sunshine to the world are probably Jewish, perhaps most famously Sammy Davis, Jr., who was ribbed goodnaturedly by his "Rat Pack" chums for both his religion and his race (black), as well as his stature (diminutive). His lack of an eye accounted for further merriment. Nevertheless Mr. Davis could play numerous musical instruments in a virtuoso fashion, as well as being an excellent mimic. The grace and charm with which he submitted to the ribbings in question attests to the class and style of the Jewish people. Furthermore, no one who has seen the episode of the *Dick van Dyke Show* wherein Rob Petrie's Jewish sidekick Buddy Sorrel belatedly receives his "Bar Mitzvah" (a Jewish celebration of manliness) can fail to be moved to laughter—and tears. Indeed, one may account for the looming presence of the Jewish population in *Boyle County Ghosts* by consideration of their traditional closeness to mysticism and God. Such was not Miss Hope's stated conclusion. Rather, she tended to "demonize" her Jewish subjects through the implication that they were demons.

Yet before we rush to judgement, we must remember that today's modern "political correctness" was not prevalent in the lifetime of Esther Leland Hope. Perhaps that is a good thing! From my understanding of it, "political correctness" is a sorry state of affairs.

Am I saying, then, that Esther Leland Hope's description of the Jews is justified? Probably not. All I am saying is, it is not nice to pick on an old woman! Especially one who has been dead for many years! How would you like it if somebody picked on your dead grandmother? You probably would not like it! Even if she had controversial notions that would be termed "hate crimes" in today's strange world of "political correctness"! Esther Leland Hope is not a relative of mine, I am just using that as an example.

Chapter Five
On the Trail of Ghostly Treasure!

I first ran across the concept of lycanthropy quite by chance, when I was in the "New Age" section of the library, looking up my horoscope. I was on a break from my more serious researches at the time. I began to become uncomfortable at the numerous symptoms of lycanthropy I seemed to share with real-life lycanthropes.

Fingernails and toenails long and dirty—yes. Aversion to bathwater—yes. Shagginess of facial and/or body hair—yes. Likes to hang around graveyards—as we have seen, this is where my love of history began. Fascinated by corpses—yes and no. I find nothing especially noteworthy about the thought of corpses, but I ask you to consider my preferred choice of food, barbecue. Is it not said that pig flesh resembles most closely the taste of human flesh? I am pretty sure I have read that somewhere. Also, no food other than ribs—my personal favorite—is so openly anatomical and corpse-like. One eats said ribs directly off the bone! The only symptoms of lycanthropy that I did not exhibit were growling and barking. I could not help but wonder if it was just a matter of time.

My dreams—or should I call them nightmares?—concomitantly became more ominous (another sign of lycanthropy). My wife has informed me on more than one occasion that there is nothing more boring than other people's dreams, but that is a gamble I am willing to take.

One night, before retiring, I enjoyed a Dean Martin film on television. That night in my dreams Dean Martin reappeared, this time as the evil conductor of a dance band. He overheard me making fun of some of the lyrics of Cole Porter (I cannot remember which) and began chasing me with a straight razor. My fear was palpable.

I am no psychologist but it was clear that my unconsciousness was recommending an immediate change of scenery. Luckily a side investigation, to take place in nearby Newberry, had been suggested by my recent researches.

In its role as county seat, Newberry has much to recommend it. Numerous restaurants and a wax museum. The nondescript balloon-frame house of Lyle Francis Peters, the humble sporting goods clerk who most notably assassinated the governor. It is also the home of Woolridge, a prestigious private college founded by Methodists and attended by my sister-in-law. But perhaps most importantly Newberry played host in historical times to "the miserly old man of Newberry," a figure drenched in mystery.

As we have seen in the previous chapter, I originally viewed Miss Esther Leland Hope's tome of ghost stories as a simple research tool to add some excitement and "color" to my sketch of local remembrances. It was not the "miserly old man," however, but his buried treasure—pearls and rubies torn from the gazelle-like necks of possibly hundreds of Christian virgins—which presented itself to me as a welcome distraction from my increasingly persistent fears of becoming a lycanthrope.

Around the middle of the 19th century there lived in Newberry a wizened fellow who bit off his own tongue rather than reveal the secret location of his buried treasure. After that he was hanged by a mob, as was the custom at the time. People say you can still hear him around the old oak tree going Woo Woo Wooooo. In death, as in life, he is tongueless.

Nobody believes such rot in our modern times. The more material aspects of this classic folktale, however, naturally held some allure. In other words, I determined to locate the legendary treasure.

The benefits of my plan would be multifarious.

Riches, for example, would allow me to pay off my various debts. I could then start a "new life." The element of personal, or "spiritual," satisfaction also played a part. By finding the treasure I would convince myself that I had a purpose on this earth. Such a thrilling "twist" would also greatly increase the chances of my book being published and then my father-in-law would look like a big braying jackass with egg all over his braying jackass face. When he approached my big new home to eat crow and beg me for money to buy a fishing boat, I would see him on the security monitor and push a button, electrifying the fence. But none of these dreams could come true without the serious application of some "elbow grease."

Said grease I soon found myself to be blessed with in ample supplies!

Chapter Six

Newberry: The County Seat of Boyle County

It is possible to travel quite cheaply from South Preston to Newberry if one is prepared to spend ten to twelve hours traversing the 40-odd miles in question. A combination of public transportation, walking, and sneaking onto shuttles meant for the elderly and the handicapped will do the trick if the journey is meticulously planned—but were I to elucidate the subject fully, the result would be an entire new volume for the reader to enjoy!

Suffice it to say that I arrived in Newberry at about 10 in the evening. The weather was clammy, as befitted the ghostly purpose of my mission. I found myself near the Woolridge dormitory, where there had been a recent bomb threat or fire drill. Freshfaced co-eds, many caught unawares in their "PJs" sprawled on the cool, damp concrete, smoking clove cigarettes, giggling amiably and rubbing their bottoms against the curb.

I wandered among them for a spell, hoping against hope that I might spot my sister-in-law, a graduate student in the field of "visual anthropology." She did not live in the dorms, but in an apartment somewhere nearby. Perhaps, I thought, she might have come over to see what all the "hubbub" was about, and we would run into one another by chance!

As I was pondering these thoughts a googly-eyed security guard grabbed me roughly by the arm. He was possessed of a scraggly black moustache which did him no favors. His smell was oniony.

State your purpose he declared officially.

I am a historian doing research I reported dutifully.

I was then led to a small room where remarks were made about my long, shabby raincoat.

I am sorry you do not like it. It is the nicest raincoat I can afford I vouched.

It makes you look like a deviant he claimed. And why don't you trim your beard if you want to look decent.

You sound like my wife I countered.

I am not your wife he emphasized. In this room YOU are MY wife.

I am surprised by your analogy I stated.

Don't get uppity with me he remarked. I don't give a expletive about your two-dollar words.

At this point another, larger, gentleman entered.

What the hell are you doing, Bernie? he inquired.

Questioning a suspect my captor replied.

On suspicion of what? his superior wished to ascertain.

Terrorism came the startling conclusion.

The larger fellow grabbed up the smaller one and cuffed him severely about the ears. I could sense at once that they shared a psychological relationship.

Apologize to the man commanded the victor.

Bernie sniveled indulgently.

I am sorry about Bernie the large man vowed. He ain't right in the head. We keep him around cause he's so good-looking, ain't that right, Bernie?

Bernie did not reply.

The larger man feigned a swat at him, causing Bernie to cringe in a humorous fashion.

If you give me twenty dollars I can let you go this massive brute informed me.

Twenty dollars is a lot of money I pleaded.

Terrorism is a serious charge he explained.

Fair enough I conceded, handing him the sum he had requested.

He held the bill up to the light.

You are free to go he declared.

It was time for plan B. Apparently I would need some "inside dope" in order to find the buried treasure.

The large man directed me to a payphone next to the drugstore across the street. He stood in the doorway of his windowless shack, watching me go.

Don't be too hard on Bernie I called. He was only trying to do his job.

The door closed, followed by sounds of thrashing.

I am not in South Preston anymore! I remarked, humorously paraphrasing *The Wizard of Oz.*

Chapter Seven
History Comes Alive

It would take more than a run-in with "Johnny Law" to thwart today's modern historian! The time had come for me to mature from the dry papery cellars of libraries and archives and to embrace my investigations willy-nilly, in the "real" world. History is not just about the weird undergarments of our misguided grandmothers! In the hands of an expert, history becomes a living, breathing engagement with the eternal verities of life.

I was on the actual streets of Newberry, the very city where the miserly old man with the treasure had lived. History was something I could breathe in the air! How weak, how silly, how DEAD, seemed the pages of a musty old Sears catalog to me at that moment! As a real man in the real world—and a town with which I was all too unfamiliar—I needed the assistance of a flesh-and-blood "Dr. Watson," someone who knew Newberry like the back of her hand, someone who could share in the excitement and riches of my imminent discovery.

Luckily, and quite by chance, I had the cell phone number of my sister-in-law on a scrap of paper in my raincoat pocket. Of course! She would be the perfect person to call. Why didn't I think of it before? Thank goodness when I had removed some cash from my wife's purse for my trip, I had accidentally grabbed Sheila's number as well. (Sheila is the name of my sister-in-law.)

I punched in her number. For some reason my heart was beating.

Hello she answered.

I hung up the phone.

I have never seen so much sweat as my hands were sweating at that moment. Perhaps I had not adequately prepared my presentation! Perhaps a hunt for buried treasure would seem archaic and preposterous to an educated young woman of today's modern world!

I believed myself to be having a heart attack but with some patience I calmed down and picked up the receiver again.

I decided to emphasize her budding expertise in the field of visual anthropology, and to explain that I needed people like her on my team. I thought I might remind her of Thanksgiving dinner five or so years before, when she had been the only one who had seemed to evince an appreciation of my historical endeavors. Fixing all this firmly within my brain, I again placed the call.

Hello Sheila, it is me, Willie.

Was that you who called before she queried.

No I replied deceivingly.

What's happened, is something wrong?

No there is something very right I countered.

Where are you? Amy is out of her mind with worry.

Is Amy there? I quizzed.

What? No. I assume she's at home unless she's out combing the streets. Where are you? It says "unknown caller."

Sheila, I have noticed that your sweat does not even stink I commented. In fact it smells like flowers! I would gladly drink a glass of your sweat I continued.

At this juncture the telephone suffered a disconnection.

Chapter Eight
Newberry's Historic Taverns: A Brief History

Tavern comes from the Latin word TABERNA, or "shed." In historical times, such "taverns" were situated along the main roads so weary stagecoach travelers could stop and rest their weary bones. It is fitting, then, that I found a small tavern, a quaint if dirty place below street level, in which I could sit and contemplate the temporary confusion in which I found my plans. In the meantime I enjoyed a few rusty nails, which are a historical combination of scotch and drambuie. The place was less than busy. Its clientele seemed to consist of old neighborhood men, men who still wore hats, men of dark but undefined ethnic extractions, with the exception of three young whites who played a large number of what I would term "hypno" songs upon the jukebox. These were wordless tunes, though "tune" is a kind way to put it, full of repetitive thuddings and drawn-out electrical noises.

As I imbibed, I perused the back of the menu, which was full of historic tidbits. This particular tavern had been founded in 1950 by a man whose parents came from Lebanon, dreaming of a better future.

In time I sauntered to the jukebox and discovered to my astonishment that unlike the jukeboxes of our forefathers it was hooked up to the internet. Further study of its many labels informed me that this "internet jukebox" would play "virtually any song in the world." Typical! With an infinite selection of God's greatest gift to man—music—these youths had opted for what sounded to me like the death throes of mentally deranged robots. Lack of imagination is a telling sign of today's emotionally bankrupt youth. Or perhaps their "music" was intended to drive the "oldsters" from the place so they could have it to themselves in a sign of youthful selfishness.

Undeterred I fed the machine the two dollars it required. For ONE SONG! I regarded the booth full of youths and determined that they were gawking. Look at that fat old freak trying to be "with it" I interpreted as the content of their thoughts.

Let's see what you've got I challenged the machine aloud.

I admit that I did not know whether to be triumphant or chastened when this technological genie of melody granted my deepest wish by allowing me to select "The Dream Police" by Cheap Trick. Already I could feel the demonic pull of the internet, with its tawdry promise of instant gratification. But I did not allow it to wrest from me the last of my drinking money.

The collegians, I noted, persisted in "scoping me out." Hence I approached them, secretly satisfied at how perturbed they would be when my song came up and they were forced to experience some real music, possibly for the first time in their young lives.

I'm looking for my sister-in-law I announced. Do any of you know where she lives? Her name is Sheila.

You'll have to be more specific one of them asserted.

She's the tenderest girl in the whole world I proclaimed.

Oh her one of them snickered.

It was at this juncture that the college students observed me weeping with a hand over my eyes.

What's the matter mister? worried the female.

My mournfulness seemed to placate them for soon I was seated in their booth.

Perhaps I had been too harsh in my past reflections on the younger generation of today's modern times. My new acquaintance Trudy, for example, was a feminist theologian. I had not previously been aware that such a thing existed!

Young Dennis was in the midst of a dissertation upon the social history and aesthetics of wedding cakes. A man after my own heart!

Newt wrote a movie review column for *Groans 'n' Grumbles*, a prestigious local "popular culture" tabloid which was given away for free in the restrooms of area taverns and used clothing stores. He explained that his movie reviews, heavily influenced by the philosophy of Ayn Rand, were designed to "blow" the mind by their outrageous nature. He quoted at length several e-mails of angry personages whose minds had been "blown" by his Ayn Rand references—and went on to quote, furthermore, his cheekily controversial replies to those e-mails, which were, if anything, even more mindblowing than the original statements under contention and caused quite a hullabaloo on the highly influential letters-to-the-editor page of *Groans 'n' Grumbles*—said letters page being entitled with youthful insouciance, "Shove It!" I learned in fact more than I could have ever conceived about *Groans 'n' Grumbles*, a publication with which I had not previously been familiar. It was inspirational to see a youth of today so proud of his work! He also declaimed at some length upon an old Steven Spielberg movie entitled *The Lost World*. Newt's principle objection was that dinosaurs who had really been brought back to life would not behave in the fashion represented by Mr. Spielberg. The topic upset him tremendously and soon he was lost in brooding thought.

I'm a writer too I mentioned.

Newt's mind was elsewhere and he did not respond.

What kind of writer? Trudy expressed kindly.

Historian I clarified.

What are you working on? Dennis wondered.

I am looking for buried treasure I exclaimed. And I think maybe you are the fellows to help me.

Wow, we could be like the Scooby gang Trudy declared.

Are you referring to the classic cartoon series Scooby Doo? I hazarded.

My assumption was affirmed by all, amid much laughter.

I marveled aloud at the aptness of Trudy's "popular culture" reference.

For there is indeed a ghost involved I confirmed.

Everyone was in a hilarious mood, perhaps giddy with the prospect of treasure. In any case there was much gaiety and laughter as I explained my quest. Even Newt's balefulness seemed mollified! One or another of the young people would ask me to expound this or that portion of my story and I would comply, the laughter growing ever more roaring and hysterical. It is hard to say how many drinks were consumed. My new friends had switched, by this point, to rusty nails, and though I had run out of money, they insisted upon keeping me supplied with the same lubricious intoxicant. From now on, Dennis remarked at one point, holding aloft his glass, I'm going to call this a "rusty willie" in honor of you.

His proposal was met by screaming laughter.

Were they laughing "at" me or laughing "with" me? It is a common distinction, but a useless one. The overall feeling was one of pleasantness, though perhaps, looking back, tinged with mockery. Nevertheless there hardly could have been a more apt illustration of the phrase "a good time was had by all."

Suddenly my song came up on the jukebox. I had forgotten all about it.

This is me! I cried.

Imprecations were voiced to the Son of God by my newly minted comrades as I proceeded to regurgitate what seemed to be a troublesome quantity of bile onto my raincoat.

Chapter Nine
Murder in the County Seat!

The next thing I recall I was back at street level, admiring the way in which the streetlights of Newberry seemed to waver and bend like special effects in a film about time travel.

Perhaps I expressed the notion that time travel could be the historian's best friend—or his worst enemy. At any rate I burst into song: a spontaneous composition of my own on the subject of time travel. Both music and lyrics are lost to me now.

As I lurched about, singing loudly, I was steadied by Dennis and Newt, each of whom firmly grasped me by an arm. I believe they were trying to ascertain the location of my car, and I was attempting to explain that my car had broken down in July of the previous year and I had not been able to afford to have it repaired. A blurrier memory comes to me now in a burst of regretful shame: that of trying to "French" my new friend Trudy, who, as I seem to recollect, reacted with understandable revulsion to the unattractive characteristics I had recently accrued—not the least of which being my unkempt beard, sour as it had become with the fruits of my drunkenness.

At some point I was handed over to the authorities.

One or two doses of ipecac and several mugs of hot black "java" later a pair of lantern-jawed investigators had me in the brightly lit interrogation "box" to "sweat me" as I knew to be the chosen parlance of police detectives. What follows is my attempt at a fairly accurate transcript of the interview.

GOOD COP: Do you know why you're here, Mr. Dobbs?

ME: Drunk and disorderly?

GOOD COP: No, but that's a fine guess. I admire your grasp of the terminology.

BAD COP: Oh yeah, we got you on D-and-D, creep. How's that for terminology? You puked on three witnesses. But that's small potatoes, Puke Boy.

GOOD COP: Easy, [Bad Cop]. Mr. Dobbs isn't under arrest.

BAD COP: Yet.

ME: What is this about?

BAD COP: Ha ha ha! That's a good one! (*He kicks a chair.*) Ever heard of murder?

ME: Yes, I've heard of it.

BAD COP: Oh! We got us a college boy!

GOOD COP: You see, Mr. Dobbs, why my partner is upset is... we're investigating a particularly gruesome killing.

BAD COP (*slapping his hands on the table*): And that makes us kind of cranky!

GOOD COP: You're from South Preston, Mr. Dobbs? What's the matter with your lips? Are they dry? Are you parched from all that heaving? Would you like [Bad Cop] to fetch you a soda? Or perhaps some orange juice?

ME: Orange juice would be good.

BAD COP: Aw, [Good Cop]! You telling me I got to fetch this dirt ball an orange juice? A expletive ORANGE JUICE?

GOOD COP: Do it. And watch your language. Mr. Dobbs is here to help us.

Exit Bad Cop, muttering.

GOOD COP (*making sure he's gone*): He's a handful, isn't he?

ME: He reminds me of my father-in-law.

GOOD COP: Ha ha ha! Father-in-law. That's a good one. I have to remember that.

ME: Ha ha ha! He really does!

GOOD COP: Ha ha ha!

ME: You're nice.

GOOD COP: I think you're nice too.

Silence.

GOOD COP: Do you have any kids, Mr. Dobbs?

ME: No, just a wife.

GOOD COP: Well now you see, I'm just the opposite. I have kids and no wife. She died.

ME: I'm sorry.

GOOD COP: Thanks. Me too. But here's the thing. When I'm away from the kids at this time of night they worry about me. My oldest,

Becky… would you like to see a picture?

ME: Sure.

He takes out his wallet and shows me a picture.

GOOD COP: She's fifteen now, she's old enough so I don't have to hire a babysitter every time I go out on one of these late calls. She can look after the little ones. But they worry, you know? And I don't like leaving them alone this time of night.

ME: I'm sorry.

GOOD COP: Well, thanks. It's not your fault. I'll tell you, though. You could really help me out.

ME: What can I do?

GOOD COP: You could tell us what you know about the murder—I'm not saying confess, I mean just tell us what you know—then you could get some sleep and I could go home to my precious little babies.

ME: Did somebody die?

Bad Cop bangs through the door with a folder but no orange juice. He throws the folder on the table and Good Cop picks it up.

ME: Where's my orange juice?

BAD COP: Expletive the expletive orange juice. We've got you, you son of a expletive. Your fingerprints are all over that room.

ME: What room?

GOOD COP (*glancing up from folder*): I'm afraid this doesn't look good, Mr. Dobbs. I'm afraid we're going to have to arrest you.

ME: For what?

GOOD COP: For the murder of Bernard Harvey.

I am arrested.

ME: Should I contact a lawyer?

GOOD COP: Do you have one?

ME: No.

GOOD COP: Maybe you could call your father-in-law and he could get you a lawyer.

ME: I don't want to call him.

GOOD COP: I didn't think so. Anyway, calling a lawyer is the first sign of guilt.

ME: But I'm not guilty!

GOOD COP: Then do you really need a lawyer?

ME: I guess not.

I am shown a picture of the murder victim, who turns out to be the googly-eyed security guard who questioned me in the shack.

ME: Oh!

BAD COP: Oh! Now it's all coming back to you! Funny how a little thing like garroting a expletive dwarf can slip your mind, ain't it?

ME: I recognize this man, but I didn't kill him. Was he killed?

BAD COP: Nah, he's just restin' his peepers! He's all tuckered out after his big day at the circus!

GOOD COP: He was last seen with someone fitting your description, Mr. Dobbs.

BAD COP: How do you know him?

ME: I don't know him. He…

BAD COP: He what?

ME: He… interrogated me earlier this evening.

BAD COP: You get off on being interrogated?

ME: "Get off"?

BAD COP: You heard me. I make you itchy in your pants, sicko?

GOOD COP: Two interrogations in a single day does seem rather…

ME: Oh, I get it! Déjà vu! Ha ha ha!

Good Cop sadly shakes his head. He seems disappointed in me. I feel bad.

BAD COP: This man was a campus police officer. Poor expletive wasn't a real police officer but he was close enough in my book. You're going down for this one, punk!

GOOD COP: Why was Bernard interrogating you?

ME: Bernie.

BAD COP: Well, well, well! I thought you didn't know him, smart guy!

GOOD COP: Why was Bernie interrogating you?

ME: He… He thought I was looking at some girls.

GOOD COP: Now why would he think that?

ME: I don't know.

GOOD COP: Well now he must have had a reason. Why don't we all try to figure it out together.

BAD COP: NOW his pants is getting itchy. Thinking about them young girls, making his pants all itchy.

ME: I beg your pardon, sir!

GOOD COP: Now [Bad Cop], if you'd ease up a little maybe Mr. Dobbs could explain what he was doing at the girl's dormitory, where several witnesses place him.

ME: I was looking for my sister-in-law.

GOOD COP: Now we're getting somewhere. Does she live in the dorm, then?

ME: No.

BAD COP: Oh! But you were just looking for her there. On a wild hunch.

ME: I came to town to do some historical research.

BAD COP: Well pardon me all to hell!

GOOD COP: And when Bernie caught you doing this "historical research"...

BAD COP (*but not a nice laugh*): Ha ha ha! Historical research! That's what he calls pulling his pud!

ME: I'm not familiar with that expression, though I'm sure I can guess the meaning.

BAD COP: I'm sure you can, Pud Puller!

GOOD COP (*sadly*): I can't believe I showed you a picture of my daughter.

BAD COP: Aw, lighten up, [Good Cop]. Hell, I mean this is something we can all understand. What the hell, man. Nice, wet night, lots of squirmy college babes. It just makes your pud feel squirmy, don't it? And then you have to take it out and pull it.

GOOD COP: I think I'm going to be sick. I need some air.

Good Cop rises and makes as if he's going to leave.

ME: No! Please don't leave me alone with him!

GOOD COP: Well... I could stay...

ME: Please do.

GOOD COP: But you're going to have to be a little bit more open with us, Mr. Dobbs. I'm a little fuzzy on something. If you were behaving completely above board, as you suggest, why was it that your friend Bernie brought you in for questioning?

ME: I… I don't know. He said it was my raincoat. Where's my raincoat?

GOOD COP: Don't worry about your raincoat.

BAD COP: Yeah, we're taking REAL GOOD CARE of your raincoat!

GOOD COP: Was Bernie mean to you? Did he make fun of your raincoat?

ME: He impugned its quality. I touted its affordability.

GOOD COP: But he just didn't listen.

ME: No.

GOOD COP: Just like your father-in-law.

ME: I guess.

GOOD COP: Bernie could probably be very abrasive.

ME: Yes, he was kind of abrasive, but…

GOOD COP: Did he remind you of your father-in-law?

ME: Why do you keep asking me that?

GOOD COP: I believe it's the first time I've mentioned it.

ME: Have you talked to the other guy who was there?

BAD COP: Oh! Now there's another guy! What was his name? Santa Claus?

ME: No…

BAD COP: Jolly Old Saint Nick?

ME: That's the same as Santa Claus.

BAD COP: Kris Kringle?

ME: But…

BAD COP (*getting "in my face"*): Are you smarting off to me, tough guy?

ME: No. I just thought you were making an unusual amount of references to Santa Claus.

BAD COP: You got something against Santa Claus?

ME: No…

GOOD COP: Does he make you nervous? The way he gets the girls to sit on his lap? Does it make you feel funny inside?

ME: I don't understand how we got onto Santa Claus. I really don't have strong feelings about him one way or another.

GOOD COP (*checking his notes*): Well, I don't know. You seemed to imply that a magical elf, such as Santa Claus, was suddenly in the room with you, to defend you from Barney.

ME: Bernie.

GOOD COP: Right. You seem to know him very well.

ME: I don't know him at all! (*trying to see notes*) Can I...

Good Cop snaps shut pad.

ME: Did I say magical elf? I don't think I would have described him that way. This was a big guy...

GOOD COP: Right. This "big guy," he your special friend?

ME: I don't have a special friend.

BAD COP: Well boo hoo hoo. That's real sad. You want me to call Douglas Sirk[1] so he can make a sad movie about it?

ME: No thank you.

GOOD COP: Does this "friend" appear whenever you're in trouble? You know, like in that commercial about the leprechaun?

ME: No... But he did help me out with Bernie. Yeah, I mean, I guess he DID appear tonight when I was in trouble, but...

GOOD COP: Oh, I see...

BAD COP: Oh! The tooth fairy!

ME: No... Gosh, do you think I could get that orange juice?

GOOD COP: I'm afraid you've missed out on the orange juice. They throw out the old orange juice at two a.m. and then there's no more orange juice till tomorrow morning.

ME: Maybe some water?

BAD COP: Maybe not. Bernie won't be having water tonight. He'll never have water again! And he loved water! Damn you, how he loved sweet, sweet water!

GOOD COP: All this talk of water is making me thirsty myself! Why don't we just clear up a few things here and then we'll see if we can get you something to drink.

ME: But I can't clear anything up for you! You need to talk to the big guy.

BAD COP: The big guy.

ME: Yes.

BAD COP: Who's that? The Jolly Green Giant?

ME: No…

BAD COP: King Kong? The Muffin Man?

ME: The Muffin Man?

BAD COP: Are you busting my chops, sweetie pants?

ME: No, I'm just saying… You were… you were listing people known for their bigness and then you added in the Muffin Man, so…

Bad Cop kicks MY chair! I nearly fall out.

GOOD COP: I must admit, my patience is running thin here, too, Mr. Dobbs. Who is this big guy you keep obsessing about? Do you call him "the Muffin Man"? Is that what he tells you to call him in your head? Does he remind you of your father-in-law?

ME: No! He was some other security guy! A big guy! When I left he was knocking the little guy around. They seemed to share a psychological relationship.

Bad Cop rubs his face. Good Cop looks at Bad Cop. I seem to have said something significant. They ask a few more questions but it begins to feel desultory. I am officially booked and led to my cell.

---

[1] Douglas Sirk, 1900-1987. Director of stylish if overblown Hollywood melodramas of the 1950s, often featuring as central characters lonely persons much like myself—at least in [Bad Cop]'s estimation of me. Many contend that Sirk's personal taste and craftsmanship transcended his mediocre source materials and approached sublimity. I knew nothing of this until I got back to the South Preston Library and looked it up, but I did not wish to anger [Bad Cop] by my ignorance of his "popular culture" reference. In a strange way, and with the benefit of some distance, it made me feel rather kindly disposed toward [Bad Cop], having gained, in retrospect, this tiny window onto his humanity—namely his familiarity with (and quite possibly a hidden or psychologically unacknowledged affection for) the emotionally touching films of Douglas Sirk. History teaches us that persons are very complex!

Chapter Ten
On the Old South Preston Trail

The modernistically paved highway which runs between Newberry and South Preston covers much the same ground as the fabled Old South Preston Trail of days of yore. This trail was first carved out by the exertions of wagon wheels over its rough terrain of dirt and other old-time materials.

The Old South Preston Trail is perhaps best known for the series of male-on-male gropings that occurred on and around it in the late 18th century. This was at a time when our founding fathers thought nothing of "hitting the town" in face powder, silk stockings, an elaborate "codpiece" and a nice wig. And probably lipstick for all I know.

I stared out the window of my father-in-law's Lincoln Town Car, contemplating history. I could almost see Indians and sexual predators peeking out at me from behind the obscurity of the trees that sped past, calling out mentally, *Do not forget us, Willie Dobbs! Record our exploits so that future generations may remember us forever!*

I muttered a solemn promise to the effect.

Did you say something my father-in-law gurgled phlegmatically.

They were his first words to me. He had transacted the morning's business in utter silence, picking me up from the police station after the large security guard had confessed to little Bernie's murder, thus clearing my name. It had quickly become clear, however, by his all-engulfing and hate-filled silence, that my father-in-law had chosen to focus on the initial accusation and my admittedly slovenly appearance after a night "behind bars," rather than the happy circumstances and total vindication surrounding my release.

In any case I did not rise to the bait of my father-in-law's sneering inquisition, choosing instead to look at the historical scenery whizzing by in an ecstasy of meaningfulness.

Was this not the historian's lot? To ride along, with someone else driving far too quickly, trying in vain to make sense of this or that vague blur—now here, now vanished? Was my father-in-law, perhaps, nothing more than a fleshly symbol of grim, skeleton-faced, cadaver-devouring Time itself? I congratulated myself on the aptness of my metaphor.

Quit talking to yourself my father-in-law chattered irritably.

Seeing that I would not indulge him in a pointless argument, he redoubled his efforts to distract me from my work.

So this is it huh he challenged. I guess you're going to sit there looking out the window all the way home with your mouth hanging open like a retard. Need a bib? I think I got a bib for you in the glove compartment.

I remained silent.

You remind me of a dog I used to have. All that dog ever did was look out the window of my truck. I used to wonder what the hell he was looking at. What did he expect to see? Some other dogs? Something better than what he already had? Ha! Good luck, you dumb mutt. I used to say, Hey you dumb dog there ain't nothing out there for you. I'm the one that feeds you. If you got to look at something look at me you dumb mutt. Wasn't for me, you wouldn't eat. Here I am your meal ticket and all you can do is look out the window like you think you're hot stuff. But he wouldn't change. He couldn't understand what I was saying. That was because he had a dog brain the size of a pea. Yes sir, when the time came I shot that dumb mutt right in his dumb dog brain. Pow!

I persisted in my contemplations.

Look at you, just like a dog.

I made no outward note of the comparison, though in a disturbing resurgence of lycanthropy it briefly occurred to me that it might be fun to bark at him just to see what he would do. The simple thought of it caused me to cackle and snort—indeed to "howl" with laughter, the effect on my father-in-law being a fearful silence, which I welcomed with all my heart.

Chapter Eleven
Notable Figures of South Preston

After penning the tantalizing title of this particular chapter, my researches in the library led me to realize that there are no notable figures of South Preston. Hence rendering said chapter title ironic or moot! Perhaps Esther Leland Hope, but we have already covered her.

I am afraid that South Preston cannot take credit for Black Pete Ogilvy, the "Ravishing Bandit" whose headquarters were in Newberry, though many of his crimes took place on the Old South Preston Trail. It must be remarked, however, that "Black Pete" was eventually castrated by a group of concerned traditionalists on the outskirts of South Preston, so perhaps we have SOME small claim on him! Nonetheless the point is a technical one and as such I am loath to exploit it.

If we widen our scope to all of Boyle County, however, we will discover that the area is rich indeed with personages of grand historical import. Who can forget Lyle Francis Peters, the famous assassin who gained statewide notoriety? And there are a whole lot more where he came from!

Take, for example, the man or woman who tampered with the toilet paper in several Happy Boy supermarkets in the spring and summer of 1989. This individual, who caused massive discomfort in the area, was never caught, but he (or she!) was thought to be a disgruntled former employee of the Happy Boy chain.

But despite the advice of today's dubiously dubbed rap "artistes," crime is not the only way to get famous, as the history of Boyle County gives ample—and colorful—evidence.

First and foremost, of course, is Johannes Hubbard Boyle, the dashing figure for whom the county is named, and whose mysterious dismemberment remains a mystery to this day.

Mention must also be made of Amelia Pringle, a favorite daughter from just outside Bunt. Pringle is perhaps best known as "Chesty Lou," the pseudonym under which she pioneered the art form of reciting filthy jokes onto phonograph records. The resultant recordings were enjoyed by even the most respectable U.S. citizens in the 1950s, mainly at the sophisticated "cocktail parties" which dominated the national psyche at the time.

I also seem to remember something about a brave milkman who saved a cat, but regrettably I have misplaced that particular clipping.

Whatever happened to milkmen, by the bye? Perhaps it is THEY who are the true heroes of our epic tale! Ordinary men who rose before dawn to accomplish their task of delivering milk.

Still it is distressing for a historian to realize that he has run out of famous personages about whom to scribe.

Alas, worldly accomplishments are elusive—and even when attained, transitory.

One night, by way of example, I viewed a particularly glorious Cheerios commercial. It was more like a slice of real family life than a commercial. The father and son were depicted with a tender, even noble, naturalism. The shot of the product itself was infused with an almost metaphysical subtlety—a single cheerio, perfectly crisp and whole, aloft in an infinite, smooth universe of milk. It was, I perceived with complete assurance, the greatest Cheerios commercial ever made.

I wondered if, when they were done "shooting" said commercial, the fellow in charge had opined, Boys, we have just made the greatest Cheerios commercial of all time. And then up went a mighty cheer.

In a way it was something to be proud of. In another way it was not.

It was, perhaps, from God's point of view, imperceptibly different from the WORST Cheerios commercial ever made.

In other words, perhaps I should have stuck with my original intention. A History of the United States is something you can sink your teeth into! What would God think, on Judgement Day, of my humble history of South Preston? To Him it would probably appear like the history of a turd.

It was at this juncture, in the midst of these gloomy and self-critical inward pronouncements, that the obvious occurred to me: Why could not I, Willie Dobbs, become a notable figure of South Preston? On this count I had more going for me than most, taking, if you will, a double-fisted shot at immortality—first as the author of a breezy local history in the "populist" vein and secondly as the discoverer of a buried treasure. Even if I failed at one of these endeavors I would assuredly succeed at the other. The law of averages guarantees as much!

It was at this juncture that I happened upon the ingenious *coup de grace* of changing my title from *The Trash Birds of South Preston (and other amazing true facts about America's friendliest town!)* to *The Mysterious Secret of the Valuable Treasure.* Normally I do not approve of such changes. Revision and "rewriting" are, to me, signs of weakness or low self-esteem in a writer. I highly doubt that the great authors of the past, such as William Faulkner and Isaac Asimov, spent their free time in such a piddling and self-indulgent fashion.

Yet by impulsively placing South Preston in my title, I had immediately cut my potential audience by several billion of the world's population. By emphasizing my role as treasure-seeker, however, I could exploit the international fascination with seekers of treasure. I am sure that the Bedouin roaming the desert and the Aborigine shooting animals with poison darts would be as delighted to find treasure as the Midwestern farmer plowing his field or the Southern aristocrat sipping mint juleps with his faithful bloodhound.

In literature, the reader often "identifies" with the hero about whom he (or she!) is reading. And the longing for buried treasure is among the most basic of human emotions! By merely changing my title I had rocketed my future book from the musty provenance of the "Regional Interest" section to the more compelling displays at the front of the store, where delectable real-life dramas are stacked in attractive and eye-catching piles.

It was at this juncture that I began to develop my theory of literature.

In my many lolled hours in the environs of reputable bookshops, libraries and archives I had noticed that far too many books have been published for anyone to actually read.

My natural conclusion was that the publishing industry should have shut down years ago, having surfeited its pragmatic usage. It is, quite simply, the law of *caveat emptor*, known more colloquially as "supply and demand."

And yet the publishing houses, alone among the great bastions of capitalism, consistently ignore the fact that no one wants their product. These great heaping mounds of hardbacks, 30% off, 40% off, like piles of rotting fruit in an exotic bazaar! To use impeccable logic, publishers should subsidize authors for NOT writing, so that the overwhelming surplus of literature could be brought, eventually, under control. Therefore as you can see,

I had determined by my own thoughtfulness that as there is no USE or PURPOSE for new books to come out, there must—*ipso facto!*—be a secret trick to getting published. A wink, a clever handshake, a cabal.

Now that I had cozened it out by pure, cruel logic, did that not qualify me for entry into the sect? I could easily imagine myself at a "black tie" dinner in honor of Erma Bombeck or Gore Vidal, "talking the talk" with the best of them!

I am afraid that I got no actual writing done for weeks to come, enraptured as I found myself by my rich imaginings of life as it would manifest itself after my book was published.

My wife, she often remarked during this period, witnessed me pacing about the house with a strange walk that she referred to as a "partial skip." Though I was unconscious of this activity, it was apparently accompanied by a bowed head and glazed-over eyes, as well as the rapid fluttering of my hands in an excitable flurry.

Willie! Willie! she would shout worriedly.

And I would realize sheepishly that I had once again become lost in thought; or rather, that I had been visiting a wonderful and magical place that seemed as real to me—no, REALLER, than the physical confines of my usual life.

In this world, to which I found myself retreating more and more, *The Mysterious Secret of the Valuable Treasure* was a "best seller." Amy had left me for another man, so that when Sheila came over with a casserole with which to comfort me, one thing naturally led to another. Now Sheila and I were off to Hollywood as advisers on the blockbuster film that was being made from my book!

The Mysterious Secret of the Valuable Treasure was directed by Clint Eastwood, who enjoyed my company so much that he invited me over to his house all the time. I would stand in the kitchen drinking a glass of red wine while Clint Eastwood expertly cut up some tomatoes. In Clint's film I was portrayed by Robert Downey, Jr. and the role of Sheila had been taken by that daughter of Goldie Hawn who looks just like Goldie Hawn.

One time Goldie Hawn's daughter and I were alone in the costuming area.

Hey remember when your Mom was on *Laugh-In* I questioned.

Goldie Hawn's daughter acquiesced.

She would wear those little bikinis and she had colorful drawings and sayings written all over her I expanded.

I wonder what I would look like in an outfit like that pondered Goldie Hawn's daughter.

Yes I was just thinking the same thing I replied.

But I am not covered in colorful drawings Goldie Hawn's daughter complained.

I think that I can take care of that I suggested. Now peel I stated assertively.

Hello my sister-in-law breathed from behind some hangers bearing gossamer clothing. Mind if I join the fun?

But there is one undeniable drawback to retreating into a fantasy world! Unless I was able to sit down and actually finish my book, none of it could ever come true! Yet the sheer entertainment value of my increasingly vivid and realistic reveries threatened to subsume me completely.

At this juncture I must thank my wife for "snapping me out of it."

One night she gently accosted me in bed.

You need professional help she remarked.

About my book? I presumed.

Yes she worried.

I think you are right I responded. I should see about contacting a professional writer. Not to help me write it, just to help me along with the business aspect. It is a fine thing to write but what's the point if you can't share it with the world through marketing techniques? This is going to be big, baby I concluded.

That's not the kind of professional help I meant she stammered.

My wife went on to explain the kind of professional help she had meant.

Our conversation on the subject was long and contentious and we fell asleep in a bewildered state.

I was shocked to awake the next morning to the scent of a delicious breakfast. My wife had stayed home from work in order to "pamper" me!

I thought you were angry I marveled.

Just worried she contradicted. And look what I found on the internet.

She showed me an adult education course offered by the Sproatsborough Art College. It was called "Finishing (or Starting) Your Masterpiece" and it would be taught by a professional writer! My wife thought that if I took the course, one of two things would happen: Either I would be exalted and encouraged or, conversely, chastened and "brought back to reality." Either way, she thought it would be an important step in my development, and I was inclined to agree.

Now you'll have to clean yourself up to participate in something like this she noted.

I acknowledged as much.

And if nothing comes of this I want you to promise me you'll at least look for a job she pressured.

Don't stifle my creativity! I screamed righteously.

She agreed not to stifle my creativity.

There is also a doctor I want you to talk to she added.

But I was engrossed in the internet and indeed had already found a similar adult education course in Newberry, a more amenable location than plain and pedestrian Sproatsborough for the fostering of one's growth as a human being.

Chapter Twelve
Return to Newberry

My adult education course was scheduled on Tuesday and Thursday nights from 8:00 to 10:30. My wife borrowed her father's car and dropped me off in Newberry for my first week of class. The plan, generally, called for a commute, but there was a celebratory aspect to this initial sally, and our three-day separation was intended as a mini-vacation for both of us. In addition to "footing the bill" for the $800 tuition, my wife had rented me a room at the Red Carpet Inn and rewarded me with upwards of a hundred dollars in pocket money.

I peeked out of the motel room window as she drove away. As soon as I had ascertained that she was gone for good, I hastened for the telephone and dialed my sister-in-law, whose number I had happened to bring with me.

Hello she purred.

I was silent.

Is that you Willie?

For some reason I could only respond to her question by breathing in a throaty and agitated manner. Perhaps I was suffering from a respiratory disorder caused by psychological causes!

I'm hanging up she avowed.

I'm lying on my bed in the Red Carpet Inn right here in Newberry I described. Can you guess what I'm doing right now I ventured.

Oh that's it she uttered melodiously. I'm telling Amy about these calls. I'm about to have lunch with her in ten minutes.

What? What? I moaned dumbfoundedly. I was just going to say that I'm busying myself by preparing for a writing class. That's what I wanted you to guess! I thought you would be happy for me because of our shared educational interests.

You call me one more time and just see what happens she warned mystifyingly.

I'm free all day Wednesday. I thought we could get together and discuss buried treasure. It's a secret project that I've revealed only to you I elaborated coaxingly. The rest of the family doesn't understand us. I need someone to discuss my urges.

This is your last chance she intoned sepulchrally and with that our call was terminated.

My CREATIVE urges I clarified to the dead air. I wondered what she had been wearing as we spoke. Perhaps something comfortable!

I continued busying myself. Soon it was time for class, which occurred in the basement of a building.

Chapter Thirteen
The Education of Willie Dobbs

As I am sure you are all aware life is about having epiphanies the impressively mustachioed writing instructor explained.

Everyone seemed to understand what he was talking about. His round wire-rimmed glasses, reminiscent of the late rock star John Lennon, were tinted yellow in what I took to be an indicator of wealth and fashionable tastes.

Sometimes I have three or four epiphanies before my second cup of coffee he went on.

Murmurings of excitement greeted this stunning announcement.

That is why it is so important to have a couple of epiphanies in your short stories he continued. Conflict is also important. I want a sandwich. Oh no! There is a bear standing between me and the sandwich. Either I defeat the bear or the bear defeats me. Perhaps as I take a bite of the sandwich the bear rips out my intestines and I have an epiphany. There in a nutshell is the essence of great writing. And that is just off the top of my head. To make it realistic we give the bear a detail, such as, I don't know. A glass eye. Suddenly he springs to life! The smell of his wet fur. Like a, like a soiled carpet that has been left in the sun. Now I am going to pass out an example of great writing for us to look at more concretely. It is a story I wrote about a man who drinks too much at a party and astonishes everyone with his epiphanies. But I don't want to give away the ending! It's a doozy.

We took turns going around "the circle" telling what we wanted to "get out of" the class.

One elderly woman wished to pen a Christian romance novel.

The instructor seemed to view this endeavor with suppressed groaning.

Another wished to collect delightful old family recipes for her grandchildren, perhaps interspersed with humorous tales of outhouses and the time the cow stepped on her foot.

A young man—the only young man in attendance, and the only male other than myself and the instructor—had written outlines for an entire series of detective novels entitled *The Gay Republican and His Gay Repub-*

lican Lover. In each volume this unlikely duo would become entangled in yet another mystery! A few of the sequels this charming and talkative young writer had in store were *The Gay Republican and His Gay Republican Lover Go to Rio* and *The Gay Republican and His Gay Republican Lover in: Murder on the Slopes*.

The entire class, myself included, expressed delight at the prospect of reading these saucy undertakings.

The instructor held a different view, which he detailed by explaining the reasons why genre fiction was beneath all of us. As an example he read some of his story about the well-to-do drinker. At the part where the gentle and wounded drunkard drops his glass into the empty swimming pool and has an epiphany our instructor whipped off his fashionable yellow "shades" and we discerned that tears had sprung tenderly into his amply creased eyes.

He soon regained his composure.

Do you know what *Esquire* said about that story? he prodded us.

Those of us who replied, replied that we did not know.

It doesn't matter. They're a bunch of ignorant losers. Any questions?

What are you famous for? someone asked.

My inability to pay child support he quipped bleakly.

Various members of the class explained that we were referring, rather, to his publications, if any, as an author.

Oh, I don't know. Have you heard of *The Tallapoosa Review*? he queried.

No we answered.

Wadded Leaves? The Oscar Homulka Quarterly? He named several other periodicals, the titles of which seemed off-putting and ill-considered and, perhaps, falsified.

One of my letters to the editor was published in *People* magazine revealed the young author of homosexual mysteries.

His classmates, including myself, were highly impressed by this news and prevailed upon him for details. Our new friend withdrew from his garments a folded and wrinkled clipping which, with delighted anticipation, we observed him unfolding and unwrinkling.

I thought some of the other letter writers were giving Drew Barrymore an extra hard time he prefaced.

Put that away the instructor demanded. We are here to discuss real writing.

What do you consider REAL WRITING challenged the insulted young homosexual.

I won the Larry O. Manfred award for juvenilia the instructor boasted triumphantly.

Much like his other mentionings, it did not ring a bell.

You weren't in *Great Stories About Horses* noted a plain though pleasant-looking lady of about 30.

What the hell is *Great Stories About Horses*? our instructor demanded. I am sorry he appended. I should have instituted some discipline right from the beginning. I should have detailed the literary objectives of this particular class. That's my own fault, and I apologize for the oversight.

Well I think the young man's notion about the queers is super neat objected one old lady. Queers are very popular right now.

We were all interested and excited by his queers someone else added.

That is just how you know an idea is crap the writing instructor maintained. The more popular it is the more crappier it is. As a rule of thumb.

His grammar was ridiculed by some of those "in the know."

I freely break the rules of grammar he argued persuasively.

Well then I guess anything goes in this day and age complained a sweet old lady.

No first you have to know the rules and only then can you break them the instructor epigrammatized marvelously. Now I think it's time for a break. Teacher is going to rest his eyes for a minute.

Everyone filed from the room toward the vending machines with various degrees of rage and disappointment.

I'm reporting you to the bursar! the young mystery writer threatened.

I don't blame you countered the instructor in the doomed tone of one who has learned from a harsh tutor known as reality to accept his fate.

But the stylish young mystery writer was not finished with him yet. Girl, I'll be a star while you're still here in your sad nasty basement he predicted.

Oh, snap! someone observed.

Snap indeed the instructor replied.

Soon the instructor and I were alone.

I am not sure I belong in this class I opened.

I am not sure any of us belong in this class he returned.

For one thing my area is history I explained. Also I believe I may be more advanced than some of the others.

What are you working on? the instructor inquired.

A History of the United States I exaggerated grandly.

Holy mackerel he chimed without enthusiasm.

I had no response for such an exclamation, shrouded as it obviously was in many complex emotions of attraction and repulsion.

I noted with some surprise that the writing instructor had fallen asleep. I watched as his head sunk to the necessary level to make it snap up again in a jarring return of consciousness.

Are you still here he wondered redundantly.

Yes I answered accurately.

He motioned with two fingers, indicating that he wished for me to approach his desk. I came forward, clutching my manuscript, and then stood by feeling quite exposed and nauseated as he flipped through the pages with impatient rapidity.

At last he looked at me.

This is composed in the florid tones of the autodidact he proclaimed unsympathetically.

A mantle I wear with pride I responded expansively.

Ha ha ha he laughed ruefully.

What's so funny I internalized silently.

You use a lot of adverbs he stated querulously.

How many is a lot I challenged calmly.

A lot is too many he returned cryptically.

I guess that's your opinion I deferred cannily.

And what have you got against the word "said" he sputtered abruptly.

I use whatever words my brain thinks are appropriate I explained patiently.

What does your brain tell you about quotation marks he lisped tentatively.

From what I have seen of history it does not use quotation marks. And from my understanding of writing James Joyce didn't use quotation marks either I trumpeted handily.

Have you read much Joyce he reproached slyly.

All of it I expounded firmly.

Finnegans Wake he pressed condescendingly.

They gave us that one in 6th grade I insisted unwaveringly.

I have nothing to teach you he admitted finally.

Chapter Fourteen
A "Night on the Town"

Thus I found myself in an enviable state. Free and loose!

The advantages were many.

Knowing that I could go to the adult education building the next morning and demand a cash refund of $800 was liberating in terms of the amount of money that I felt able to spend immediately upon alcohol and other sundries.

Perhaps more importantly I now had two whole days and nights in front of me with no obligation other than that of finding the buried treasure! Of course, familial duties would also demand that I spend as much time as possible with my sister-in-law.

Treasure and suchlike pleasantries would have to wait, however! It was far too late for a trip to the Newberry Archives. Likewise, I felt that I needed some "liquid fortification" before attempting another chitchat with Sheila.

I was delighted, upon entering my favorite saloon, to perceive the fiery young collegiate film critic Newt in a back corner, attempting to read by the dim—nay, almost non-existent—light therein.

I approached him in a spirit of camaraderie.

You'll strain your eyes I ribbed jokingly.

He looked up from his periodical, which, as I discerned at that juncture, was a copy of *Groans 'n' Grumbles*, the "edgy" underground publication for which he scribed. Taking the barest note of me, absorbed as I took it in the devastating edginess of a particularly irreverent penning, he returned to his reading without comment.

You college boys! I bantered jovially. I guess you are perusing something fairly "wild."

I am TRYING to proof my review of the new Halle Berry feature he erupted volcanically.

Hubba hubba I remarked convivially.

It is not her looks which concern me, sir, but her sexual politics. Which naturally lead to *realpolitik*! he lectured grandiosely. If you had troubled yourself to read my piece before making your condescending little smacking noises, you would know that in it (here he rattled his *Groans 'n' Grumbles*) I mount an astonishing case that Roy Cohn was the greatest American who ever lived.

I am astonished I admitted. I would have accorded that honor to Paul Revere.

He grunted at me in a way that I found it nigh upon impossible to interpret. I chose to chalk it up to youthful braggadocio, and to continue the conversation in a spirit of cheerful elan:

It may please you to know that I have been brushing up on my Douglas Sirk!

This cinematic icebreaker garnered zero recognition from the surly young genius.

Did you see the one where Rock Hudson blinded a lady I prompted. It was a corker.

You couldn't handle my controversial opinions on the matter he reputed.

It was at this juncture that I began to canvass the establishment for other companionship.

Whom should I spot slouched at the bar over a toddy of some sort but [Good Cop]? I excused myself and approached my former adversary, seating myself on the stool next to his.

There he is! I greeted friendlily.

I know you he replied, glancing over grudgingly.

Isn't it kind of late? I joshed. I thought you would be at home with your wonderful kids.

I don't have any kids.

Becky and the little ones? I rebuked.

Oh. The picture in my wallet. That's a trick we use to make you confess to stuff you didn't do.

A trick of the trade! I elaborated.

I guess so he replied.

I could tell from his expression that he was a miserable human being. Perhaps it was the contrast of his noble, imagined life—dedicated widower and father—with that of his actual life as a miserable so-and-so all alone, drinking his sorrows away in a dingy bar. In any case I was moved to buy him many drinks, which he received with good graces, including many comments of Hey chief you're all right in my book.

As for me, I downed several large water glasses filled to overflowing with Pernod and ice. As I now may attest, this is not the proper way to consume Pernod. I am afraid that I took advantage of the bartender's ignorance, allowing him to charge me for these mammoth servings what one would normally charge for a small tumbler of the vivid and chartreuse liquid. My punishment was severely manifest the next day, you may be sure! In the meantime, however, I found it lovely to watch the Pernod change colors as it hit the ice. [Good Cop] shared my interest in this odd property of the popular French liqueur.

That's some psychedelic expletive he commented.

I read about it in the library I boasted shamefully. It is too bad that absinthe is illegal. I could really go for some of that right now.

Maybe there's some in the evidence room [Good Cop] suggested.

Oh I doubt it I corrected. They outlawed it when it made Vincent van Gogh chop off his ears.

That poor jerk [Good Cop] mused thoughtfully. I saw a movie about him. Nobody appreciated him while he was alive. The world consists of a bunch of jerks! Remember the time he painted some sunflowers?

There's a young fellow over there who knows all about movies I indicated. Maybe we could talk about movies with him and that would cheer you up.

That punk? [Good Cop] barked aggressively. He thinks he knows more about movies than I do? I'll wipe up the expletive floor with him.

Let's talk about crime I suggested distractingly.

What about it.

Do you like solving it? I inquired.

It pays the bills he claimed.

I am a journalist I fudged. I have been doing some crime writing as of late. In particular I am fascinated by the Happy Boy toilet paper tamperings of 1989.

Are you getting me hammered so you can grill me for your damn scandal rag? At this juncture his undertone was rife with threat.

No, not at all. I'm a self-employed historian with no loyalty to any large media outlet. I thought you might like talking about crime to pass the time I gulped.

Poor Dan Bee he muttered.

I inquired as to the identity of this mysterious Dan Bee.

Only the greatest cop who ever lived came the intriguing reply. He caught the Happy Boy case just before he retired. It dogged his SOUL that he never found that piece of expletive. (At this juncture [Good Cop] slammed his glass on the bar in a fury.) I wish to hell I could find the "butt bandit" that pulled off that rotten job. I'd hand him to old Dan Bee on a silver platter. Happy birthday, old Dan Bee. Do with this scum what you will.

I am an awful criminal I blurted impulsively.

Come again [Good Cop] requested.

It was I who tampered with the toilet paper! I lied. It was I who ruined your friend's life!

At this juncture it would behoove me to examine why I tried to turn myself in for a crime I did not commit. Perhaps my reasons involved psychology!

It must be admitted firstly that pretending to be a famous criminal made me feel big and important. If I may be immodest, however, I believe that some more altruistic motivations were also on display. Namely, I wanted [Good Cop] to be happy! At that moment, I honestly believe, I would have done anything to gain his favor, and to soothe his troubled brow.

Was I in fact the loneliest man on earth? Did I merely crave human contact, ANY human contact, so that even the rough application of a pair of handcuffs administered by a somewhat frightening stranger might have been welcomed like a lover's gentle bussing of my eyelids?

While such is indeed a romantic speculation, it fails to take into consideration my rich and detailed human psychology. The emotions of humans are very complex!

In any case my false protestations were brushed aside with a hoarse laugh. Even through the mist of alcohol [Good Cop] was a wily judge of character!

You're okay chief was his only comment on my peculiar confession. It was as if he were reading me like a book! Indeed I felt that he appreciated my inner workings in an almost loving manner. And at that moment I may truly say I loved him back.

He gazed deeply into my eyes, and I into his.

Did you know their jukebox is connected to the internet I remarked, sensing that it was time to change the subject.

You don't say he replied.

We returned our attention to our drinks.

Yes indeed, it can play any song in the whole world I informed him.

That can't be true he disagreed.

Pretty much any song I persisted.

Can it play that one about the glowworm? he mused.

I wouldn't be surprised I answered.

Mmm he speculated.

At this juncture [Good Cop] swiveled about on his stool to visually assess the jukebox in question. By a trick of fate, the young film critic Newt happened to be passing by at the time. [Good Cop] accosted him thusly:

Hey you. Movie Boy.

Can I help you? Newt offered primly and with some disingenuousness.

My pal here would like to buy you a drink [Good Cop] asserted.

Well that's very kind but I'm expected elsewhere Newt demurred.

[Good Cop] fished in his jacket and came out with a badge. He cocked his head toward the bar with an air of authority and intimidation.

Join us he suggested firmly.

Newt approached with apparent trepidation.

What's this all about? he asked.

I'll ask the questions [Good Cop] ordered. Now park it.

Is this official police business? Newt pressed, rooted to the spot.

None of your damn business [Good Cop] reacted.

Newt seemed to consider turning to go. It was at this juncture that [Good Cop] subtly pulled back his jacket, revealing the butt of a revolver.

Going somewhere? he questioned slyly.

Apparently not Newt answered with a touch of trembling defiance.

One drink [Good Cop] invited with a suddenly relaxed demeanor.

A grasshopper? Newt suggested.

Yes if you're a girl [Good Cop] replied. Are you a girl, Seymour?

No sir.

I'm glad to hear you're not a little panty girl wearing little panties. You'll have a boilermaker and that's that.

The stage was set for a horrible event! I felt the beginnings of an emotional rash on my neck and chest. Yet it must be frankly admitted that I took some satisfaction in young Newt's evident terror, recalling as I did the "brushing off" to which he had recently subjected me.

[Good Cop] directed poor Newt in the drinking of a boilermaker, which the latter at last accomplished amidst much gagging and perspiration.

Good boy remarked [Good Cop]. My friend here tells me you know all about movies.

I'm fairly familiar with cinema Newt wheezed.

Well la-di-da came the unimpressed reply.

I really do have to go. If I don't show, people will be looking for me. Important people. The editor of *Groans 'n' Grumbles*.

Oh, a scandal rag, huh?

He has written a controversial editorial stating that homeless people smell funny and he wants me to confirm that it is controversial enough. My input is considered a high priority and if I do not appear there will be search parties organized, you may be sure.

[Good Cop] eyed me conspiratorially. Okay, you can skedaddle in just one second, Clark Kent. IF you can answer one trivia question.

Newt waited.

Okay, this is a good one [Good Cop] began. He rubbed his hands together. Okay, here it is. Ready?

Newt did not reply.

Okay, here goes. Can you guess the name of my favorite movie about a whale?

Orca? cringed Newt.

Well you got that one right. Now tell me my favorite movie about a cop.

These aren't the kind of trivia questions I'm used to Newt protested.

Go on, take a wild guess [Good Cop] encouraged. I bet you get it right!

There are a lot of movies about cops Newt observed reasonably.

That tears it! [Good Cop] cried, leaping to his feet. I'm using your alley, Mike.

The bartender responded with only the slightest nod.

Before I could grasp what was happening, [Good Cop] had secured Newt by the collar and the belt loop, and was hoisting him fiercely around the corner and out of sight.

My sublimated wishes for Newt to come to harm were bearing spectacular fruit! I felt dreadful about it.

I found my way to the back alley just in time to see poor Newt tossed roughly into a pile of bricks and garbage.

I believe in the superior man! Newt pleaded. Read my columns! You have earned this power by assuming it! I offer you my heartiest congratulations! I can tell you're familiar with *The Fountainhead* he appealed. I know you've seen *The Incredibles* he postulated. I swear I will write a well-worded column about you! he bribed.

On your knees [Good Cop] replied.

I noted that his gun was drawn.

Nietzsche! Nietzsche! Newt raved incoherently.

What's your favorite movie? [Good Cop] quizzed.

The Tingler starring Vincent Price the answer came burbling through a curtain of tears. It is a choice that raises a few eyebrows, and causes a number of minds to be blown. Please don't kill me! I have so much to give through my film criticism. I want to see my Mommy again!

I observed to my dismay that [Good Cop] had become monstrous. Sweat was cascading from him in an unhealthy manner. His hair was disheveled in the extreme. The eyes in his otherwise handsome face had taken on a serpent-like quality devoid of human feeling. His tie was unknotted in a way contrary to all rules of etiquette. His lips were curled in an alarming rictus indicative of sociopathic glee.

You never answered my question came the chilling statement.

WHAT QUESTION? Newt shrieked.

My favorite movie about a cop.

Oh God! Is it *The Taking of Pelham One, Two, Three*?

No but that's a good one. That's a real good one, actually. I'm not sure

I'd call it a cop movie. I mean, it has cops IN it... But no, I was thinking of *Madigan* starring Richard Widmark.

Yes we all love Richard Widmark I intervened. Put down the gun and we'll debate his greatest roles.

At this juncture [Good Cop] beat Newt to the ground, synopsizing thusly:

And all the time Henry Fonda was putting it to the married lady with the fancy turban! Madigan was only trying to do his job!

He then performed what seemed to be the action of bellowing incoherently in a great froth of spittle as he crushed Newt's nose bone with the butt of his revolver.

Newt lay quite still and I could observe that his beater's knuckles and firearm alike dripped with sparkling black-and-crimson blood.

And that's how we play trivia in Newberry he summarized.

Is he okay? I asked.

He'll be fine. Help me cover him up with these cardboard boxes.

I did as I was asked then stumbled toward the back door of the bar.

Where do you think you're going? [Good Cop] demanded.

Well it's been a long night I replied.

I'll tell you when it's been a long night he answered.

I observed that his gun was trained upon my person.

It was at this juncture that I felt an enveloping warmth encasing my left leg, a not unpleasing warmth which I soon realized to be a great quantity of my own urine.

[Good Cop] had produced a cell phone, upon which he spoke the following cryptic words: Mitch. I need a cherry top. Yeah, on the QT. Personal use.

It was thus that I found myself imprisoned in the back of a police car. I discerned at once that there were no handles on my doors and no means of escape.

Chapter Fifteen
Historical Sites of Old Newberry

There followed a greatly unpleasant drive through the historic environs of Old Newberry. I witnessed many sites of scholarly interest, such as the cathedral which collapsed on worshippers and the place where the fairgrounds used to be—the latter perhaps best known for an ill-fated attempt, circa 1977, at fashioning the world's longest frankfurter. Or the time the gorilla escaped and killed many. Passing mention must also be made of the horrible fire of 1980. And the clown who was abducting children. But alas I could take but little enjoyment from the passing parade of history.

At one exciting juncture [Good Cop] pulled up on the sidewalk of an all-night convenience store, narrowly avoiding a crash through the large and colorfully garbed window of that handy establishment.

He left me alone in the backseat of the vehicle as he went in to make some purchases—or, for all I knew, a robbery. As I waited for my captor to return, some skateboarding teens took note of me.

Help! Help! I have been wrongly imprisoned by a madman! I explained.

They pelted with raw eggs the window through which my desperate visage could be seen gesticulating in terror.

It was at that juncture that [Good Cop] swaggered forth from the store, a brown bag of groceries in one arm, his opposite hand brandishing his weapon in a scarifying manner. The teens, it hardly need be remarked, dispersed at once. Ironically their newfound respect for "law and order" was in this one instance egregiously misplaced!

Upon reentering the car [Good Cop] did not acknowledge me in the least. He appeared, in fact, to have forgotten me altogether, a fact which I hoped to exploit somehow to my advantage. In the meantime I observed him as he calmly applied Mercurochrome via Q-tip to his lacerated knuckles.

Suddenly, like a heavenly bolt, my sister-in-law appeared in my line of sight, floating as it were across the parking lot, her slender thighs encased in the threadbare denim cut-offs known historically by members of my generation as "Daisy Dukes." Her couture was completed by a pink T-shirt in the popular style of today's youth, emblazoned with a childishly rendered likeness of some peculiar Asian duckling and revealing much of her belly button area as well as a generous helping of impossibly long and sculpted pelvic bone (the latter exposure accounted for by the "low riding" nature of the aforementioned "Daisy Dukes"). Her charmingly prehensile toes were on delightful display thanks to a pair of "thong" style sandals whimsically bedecked with twinkling sequins along the wispy and ethereal straps. Her flowing raven tresses, however, were somewhat regrettably concealed—albeit fetchingly—by a fashionable bandana of white and black, the perfect complement to her heartstoppingly pale skin and dark liquid irises as deep as night. Her nipples were poking out.

Was this a hallucination? It was not! Although my notion that the police car had filled in a flash with her dizzying natural aromas—rising bread, and violets, and the sea, and rich, loamy potting soil—was indeed, as I knew even then, a powerful hallucination of the olfactory variety.

I pounded my fists upon the windows, screaming her name for dear life.

My sister-in-law squinted toward me. Had she recognized me? It was impossible to tell. She appeared to take a step toward the car, but the dowdyish female school chum in whose company she happened to be pulled her away. They disappeared into the store as I sobbed and screamed that blessed name. Sheila! Sheila!

Had my reasoning faculties been more intact I might have realized that my caterwauling would attract the attention of my erstwhile tormentor. Indeed he removed himself daintily from the car and opened the back door with such quiet rectitude that I dreamed fleetingly of freedom. It was at this juncture that he silenced me—and indeed my brain itself—with what I later understood to be a cattle prod.

Chapter Sixteen

Old Dan Bee: A Notable Personage of Newberry

Open up damn you you old codger! I got some of that clam chowder you like!

The foregoing are the first words I can recall with any clarity after my unfortunate prodding. As I "came to," I perceived that [Good Cop] was rapping with alacrity upon the door of a modest single-story home in a slightly shabby locale. The barking of numerous dogs supplied appropriate counterpoint to his raucous behavior. I was, it seemed, handcuffed to the railing of the porch steps leading to the shabby home in question.

The door opened, revealing an old man in a striped bathrobe of silver and red.

I brung you a present the corrupted detective blustered ungrammatically.

So I see the old man spoke with amazing dignity.

It's the case you never cracked my captor barked corruptedly. The Happy Boy toidy tamperer! Let's drown him in the bathtub and shoot him in the eye.

You've given an old man a lot to consider the old man considered quietly. Why don't we come inside and discuss it?

What about this piece of expletive the awful man objected, indicating myself.

His elder tittered wisely. I don't think he's going anywhere he remarked.

Additional cozening was required but eventually the old man succeeded in bringing his disgraceful visitor inside the house.

My thoughts were jumbled and my attempts at escape useless.

Before long the old man returned, alone. He padded toward me down the steps on gnarled and noble feet, feet invested with a certain brand of gravitas and overlain—especially about the toenail region—with a hint of mortality.

Hello I'm Dan Bee he introduced himself, unlocking my bonds with a tiny key as he spoke.

I did not tamper with the toilet paper I clarified.

I didn't think you did, son. I have my own ideas about who pulled that job but I guess we'll never know. Young man you are a right mess he appraised.

Yes sir I confessed.

Think nothing of it! came the kind rejoinder. We do not stand on ceremony in the House of Bee. You go on in there and shower off. I've got a fresh robe for you around here somewheres. In the meantime I'll give your duds a once-over in the old washing machine. Consarn that gizmo, it sure works good!

I'm afraid my pants are soaked in number one I warned.

I've seen worse he assured.

I'm afraid to come in I admitted. I'm afraid of your friend. I'm afraid if I go to take a shower as you suggest he'll be in the towel closet waiting for me and pop out and drown me in the bathtub.

No worries! my new friend warbled kindly. I clocked that rascal with a lead weight and shut him up in the cedar chest. Then I put the encyclopedia on top of the cedar chest.

With that I accepted the hospitality of old Dan Bee. His elderly eyes were fraught to their very brims with trustworthiness!

Not even a vigorous shower, however, could entirely assuage my pains and worries. Dan Bee could sense my discomfort as we sat across from one another in his small kitchen at his small kitchen table, resplendent in our matching robes, waiting for my clothes to dry. Tiny cockroaches skittered about gaily in surprising numbers.

The writing instructor—how long ago our brief friendship seemed!—had been quite strident in expounding his theory that characters should be described—one of many points upon which we disagreed. To insist, for example, that a FICTIONAL character has yellow hair rather than black seems to me the desperate cry for help of a "control freak" or similarly mentally incapacitated tyrant. But this one concession shall I make: Describe Dan Bee I will. He had many characteristics! His face, for example, appeared to be melting. His sagging cheeks in fact sagged right off his sagging face. His sagging eye sockets appeared barely able to contain his eyes, so elastic they had become with the blessings of age. Those eyes were of a gentle blue, by the bye, although one of them was of a markedly different blue than the other and appeared to be covered with a debilitating film. The kindly hair of old Dan Bee stood in marvelous puffs about his sagging scalp. He was, in short, the loveliest and wisest of old gentlemen that I had ever seen.

You look some better Dan Bee assessed of my post-shower countenance. That ain't saying much. What's eating you, kiddo?

I think your friend killed somebody I whispered.

Why he wouldn't hurt a fly Dan Bee chuckled reassuringly. He can get tough, sure, it comes with the territory, don't it? But he knows what he's doing. That hoor will wake up tomorrow with nothing but an old-fashioned goose egg to show for her troubles.

Hoor? I pondered.

It's usually a hoor Dan Bee illuminated avuncularly.

At this juncture I moaned involuntarily, the consequences of my actions—and inaction—weighing on my head like a great weight of some kind weighing on my head. The frilly silken ribbon of my mistakes and sins stretched well beyond the calamitous evening in question, terminating only, it seemed, in the womb. I suddenly felt myself smothering in amniotic fluid and swooned as a result in my rickety chair.

I can see you're under the weather Dan Bee observed. Ain't but one cure for that. What you need is some clam chowder.

He puttered kindly about the cozy room, preparing the chowder in question.

Dread engulfed me at the prospect of this kindly chowder. I was chagrined to note the untimely appearance of another of my mental processes.

Did you ever watch that show *Homicide*? I asked.

All's I ever watch is women's basketball Dan Bee revealed in his quaint and kindly fashion, setting up all the while a wondrous gay tinkling and rattling amidst his gaily shining pots and pans which clattered and rattled with a musical timbre of joy.

I remember one time on *Homicide* it was about a lady who suddenly developed an allergy to shellfish. It came out of nowhere. She spent her whole life eating every kind of shellfish and then one time out of nowhere she ate a crab and it just about killed her. She saw double and she fell on the floor. Did you ever run across anything like that in your years on the force?

Can't say that I have Dan Bee surmised. But if it was on television I'd be inclined to believe it. Don't sound like something they'd just plumb yank out of a hat. They got people that look these things up. That's all these folks do, mind you. Look things up. Wouldn't you like to have a fine job just sitting on your keester looking things up?

Dan Bee wagged his head in genteel wonder at the strange ways of the modernistic world to which he had become a kindly and wondering stranger. I knew just how he felt!

Well what if I developed a deadly allergy to shellfish right this minute I demanded. You must admit it is possible. What if that clam chowder, however kindly offered, killed me dead?

Dan Bee gave out with another of the comforting chuckles upon which I felt myself beginning to rely like life's blood or mother's milk.

I don't think you need to worry about that he concluded.

Yet my soul was not restful.

This could be the night I predicted ominously. The one night I get an allergy to shellfish. And then I'd be dead and there wouldn't be anything anybody could do about it.

That's what dead is Dan Bee pointed out. Now what's all this fuss? This is the finest clam chowder you will ever taste. I've been eating this same clam chowder for eighty-seven years and I've never been sick once.

It was as if Dan Bee could see right through me! Down into my very soul, past my phony fears and negligent heart rattling like a piece of loose black gravel in the hollow cavity of my inner being! He was, in short, the exact opposite of my father-in-law, and I felt as if I was home—HOME!—for the first time in centuries. I could hide nothing from old Dan Bee!

Oh Dan Bee I have many problems I confessed. I have never told anybody about my disturbing mental thoughts.

This old coot for one would love to hear them he consoled.

Thusly encouraged, I gushed forth thusly: These things we're talking about now—these are the kinds of things I think about ALL THE TIME, Dan Bee! Hypochondria is a definite sign of mental deterioration. Soon I will be sealed up in a cork-lined room helplessly remembering my childhood memories and too weak and demoralized to get out of bed just like

Marcel Proust.

Oh, pshaw! Dan Bee replied. Nothing wrong with you a spanking wouldn't cure he added with a merry twinkle in his milky eye.

He then pretended merrily to try to persuade me to open my robe so he could administer the spanking to which he had referred. Despite his aged condition he even took the trouble to "chase" me about the kitchen table "demanding" that I present my bare buttocks for the spanking I "deserved." He soon tired of his playful prank and fell into a peaceful slumber, his head upon his humble table and his beloved roaches scurrying about.

Horses, it has been prominently hypothesized, should not be changed midstream. Nonetheless, upon hearing Dan Bee's plainspoken and whimsical advice, inspiration struck me that my book might soon become a different type of bestseller than I had originally intended—namely, one of those delightful tomes in which a young man encounters a wise old soul whose creaky ways belie a youthful heart bursting with rambunctious *joie de vivre.* Was Dan Bee, perhaps, my Morrie of *Tuesdays with Morrie* fame? Yes, I noted at once, he was.

Chapter Seventeen
The Treasure Trail Heats Up!

The phone woke me. I was then stabbed in the eyes by yellow sunlight, piercing like a tribe of wondrous bees through the worst hangover that the world had ever known.

Hello I croaked.

Hi honey my wife replied. I miss you. I know we're supposed to be on a break, but I was curious about your class. How did it go?

Dandy I answered. You could have knocked that teacher over with a feather when he got a load of the wild stuff I was laying down. He sat right there and told me to my face I was a better writer than James Joyce. Isn't that great news? He said, Move over, James Joyce! There's a new talent on the horizon, and the name of that talent is Willie Dobbs!

Well that's great sweetie. You just stick with it and do whatever the teacher says. I'll see you Friday morning. And then you'll see that doctor like you promised.

I sat up swiftly, revivified by the thought of the cool $800 I planned to extort from the adult education administration that very morning. The motel room spun and danced in a flurry of stars and flame.

Oh mercy I exclaimed.

Are you okay my wife worried.

Yes I just have a lot of homework to take care of I lied.

And you'd tell me if you were in the back of a police car last night she stated.

I have to go now I replied and hung up the phone.

I then retired to the bathroom for a session of retching. Afterward I lay with my head against the cool tile and slowly the events of the previous night returned to me, causing multifarious complications in my waking mind.

Some hours later I found myself able to rise. I made it to the window of my room and gazed out into the parking lot. The police car was not where I had left it. A vague and comforting inkling came over me that the night had never happened. Though aware that this inkling was erroneous, I nonetheless found it captivating.

A quick check of my wallet revealed a lone five-dollar bill. I dressed with quavering hands. It was now imperative, despite my weakened condition, that I get to the adult education building and woo a kindly receptionist or underling out of my refund posthaste. It occurred to me that I should not have spent all my money in a single night without making sure beforehand that such a refund would be forthcoming.

Alas such a refund was not forthcoming.

Such a refund, they explained, could be mailed to my wife within six to eight weeks if I filled out the proper paperwork and got her to sign it in the presence of a notary public. This offer I declined, as I did not wish to disappoint my wife with the realization that the writing class she had paid for was useless to me.

Having spent four dollars and fifty cents on my cab ride to the adult education complex, I returned to the hotel on foot, gathered my luggage, and visited the lobby.

I would like to check out early I explained.

Very well sir came the accommodating response. Will that be on the same credit card?

Yes I replied. And I would like the balance in cash.

I am sorry sir, that is not possible. Would you still like to check out?

Yes I again replied, not wishing to seem like a fool.

Thus were my plans thwarted. I had intended to use the remainder of my motel credit to rent a private car, perhaps a white limousine, in which to be driven around doing historical research. I could, I reasoned, sleep in said car, or at the home of old Dan Bee, or perhaps "crash" on the couch of my sister-in-law, or perhaps my sister-in-law would like to take a ride in a fancy limousine. In any case, I would have a little pocket money—said pocket money being the most immediate objective. What I truly craved was some Lipton's Cup-a-Soup and a package of saltines.

I notice your little set-up of sugar cookies and water I told the clerk. May I?

No sir, those are reserved for guests he replied. Which you no longer are.

I'll give you fifty cents I tempted.

Money is not the issue sir. The issue is one of policy. Of standards.

May I sit in your lobby until my ride comes? I requested.

If you must the clerk compromised.

I called my wife on the payphone.

Can you come get me? I asked. I believe I have hepatitis I remarked.

Hepatitis? How do you know?

It is just a feeling I have.

Well you stay put and I'll be there as soon as I can.

I knew I could count on you I closed.

It was at this juncture that I made a fateful discovery concerning the treasure.

Whilst talking on the phone, I had been fingering several brightly colored brochures designed to encourage tourism in the surrounding area. Imagine my delight in noting that one of these pamphlets advertised a "Haunted Ghost Walk Tour" of historic Newberry! This was my first solid clue about the location of the legendary miser I had been seeking for so long. My greatest nemesis! And the key to all my dreams!

No specific mention of misers as such was made in the brochure, but I knew that any "Haunted Ghost Walk Tour" worth its salt would include the story of the fearsome molester of Christian lasses who bit off his own tongue! Why such a tale is irresistible to the child in all of us! I regretted to note that a ticket purchase of thirty dollars would have entitled me to a place in this intriguing tour—and perhaps the solution to the enthralling mystery. Happiness, wealth, fame, aesthetic satisfaction, revenge against the doubters who had doubted me since infancy—all this and more a mere thirty dollars away!

Alas I had squandered my allowance buying drinks for a murderous thug who hid behind his badge of honor. Let that be a lesson for aspiring scribes! Frugality is prudent! Keep a spare twenty tucked in your shoe for emergencies. Or a spare thirty!

On the plus side I would surely be back in town next week for my phantom "writing class." But little did anyone know that it was another kind of phantom I would be stalking! A phantom with riches aplenty!

Chapter Eighteen
South Preston: A Hotbed of Politics

When the Lincoln Town Car arrived my wife alas was not behind the wheel. Rather it was the owner of the car, her father, whom she had sent to pick me up in her stead.

You owe me big time he grouched. I'm supposed to be golfing with Tim Willis.

Where's Amy? I asked.

Where she always is, working her fingers to the bone to support her deadbeat husband. The only blessing I can see is that you two never had children.

Doctors say my sperm is too hot I informed him.

My father-in-law shook his head insultingly. We drove for awhile in silence until he could contain himself no longer:

Amy says you're out here working on some kind of business deal. Is that true? I pray to God it's true. Although I'd be inclined to think whoever hired you was a moron of the highest caliber.

Can we stop by McDonald's? I asked.

You got any money he countered. Let me guess.

I do not I made plain.

Then the answer is no he finalized. You have to pay your own way in this world, mister. I'm aware that's a new concept for the likes of you. You make me sick he footnoted.

My stomach turned over again and again.

So, am I really supposed to believe you have some kind of business prospect on the horizon? he repeated.

Yes I prevaricated.

Would it be too much to ask if you would let me in on the big secret? he nagged.

If you must know I am running for mayor of South Preston I announced. I'm sorry you made me spill the beans. I wanted it to be a surprise. For your birthday.

Well now I've heard anything. I have to laugh to keep from crying he exaggerated. There's not an election for two years is there? You're full of horse puckey. Do you take me for a boob? Are you trying to push my buttons?

No I'm not. I am approaching this matter in all dead seriousness. I need a lot of time to gear up my campaign. I'm running on the socialist ticket I added nonchalantly.

I must admit that at this juncture I was just trying to "get his goat." And get it I did. His seething was palpable although he tried to hold it in.

I almost believe you he reported with mock calmness.

You should believe me. I have decided to believe in socialism.

I just about believe you. I believe you would do it just to bring one more shame on my head. I think you would do it to see if you could drive me into the grave with shame.

I'm doing it over my strongly held beliefs in socialism I specified.

I will give you one thousand dollars in cash to leave my daughter for good he contended evenly.

Let's start with a two cheeseburger "extra-value" meal and see where it goes from there I bargained.

Your breath smells like a sewer he noted.

I forgot to brush my teeth I confessed.

Where the hell did you spend the night he wrangled. In a sewer? he supposed.

What about that one thousand dollars I reminded.

I could just as easily take that one thousand dollars and pay someone to kill you he reasoned. If you tell Amy I said that I'll deny it.

Are you threatening me? I surmised.

You bet your boots he grinned maniacally.

Chapter Nineteen
Another Visit with Old Dan Bee

Almost a week later, on the following Tuesday afternoon, I found myself again at the home of my mentor, the amazing force of life known as Dan Bee.

What wisdom do you have to relate to me today, Dan Bee? I supplicated.

Did you bring me some clam chowder? he asked.

Yes it is bubbling on the stove right now I indicated.

Well it's nice to have company whoever you are he kidded.

You know who I am, old Dan Bee! It was your remarkable example that led me to take the exciting steps I am here to tell you about! Old Dan Bee, I am going to make both of us rich.

Did you bring me some clam chowder? he asked.

Oh Dan Bee! You are "too much!" I guffawed.

I served the chowder in question, first blowing upon it by means of my own breath in order to cool it—such was my level of endearment for this ordinary common-sensical old working class man! I enjoyed watching him slurp his chowder with an unseemly relish excusable in one of his advanced years.

How was it? I asked.

How did you get in my house? he replied, chowder splashing from his mouth with gay abandon.

You invited me I reminded him. I called you on the telephone.

Oh, it's you, Spanky! he crowed.

It's me, Willie Dobbs I corrected.

I'm going to call you Spanky he vowed.

That is fine with me! I laughed. A man of your achievements in the field of living can call me anything he wishes!

You remind me of Spanky he confirmed. Do you know Spanky?

I have never known anyone of that name I answered.

Are you Spanky's oldest? he asked.

It's me, Willie Dobbs I repeated.

What can I do for you, Spanky? he offered.

There are four things you can do for me, Dan Bee. First of all you can use your expertise to gather together a crack team of ex-soldiers and ex-policemen, and perhaps ex-firemen—you would know better than I. This team must be capable of digging up a treasure. I have recently come into a thousand dollars, so I am willing to spare no expense for the best men you can find. Tonight I am to rendezvous with an expert on treasure, so I should know more tomorrow morning. I will check in as soon as possible with the updated information, perhaps including the precise location of our buried treasure.

Dan Bee evinced no response to my exciting proposition.

We're going to be rich, Dan Bee! I prompted.

Good he replied.

There was much wisdom in his pithiness.

Now the next thing I want you to do is help me to write a book—a History of the United States. Or a history of South Preston, or Boyle County, I am not completely decided. In any case I need your wisdom, old Dan Bee. I need your wisdom like all "get out!" My thesis all along has been the gentler times of playing with marbles and painting fences and such, of which I have no personal experience. I would like to tap you for your wondrous recollections of a simpler time. Does that sound good, Dan Bee?

Sound good replied Dan Bee.

Marvelous! I cheered. Which brings me to the second book. Right now I'm leaning toward *Chattin' with Chowder*. Do you like that title, Dan Bee?

I like chowder declaimed old Dan Bee.

Boy oh boy! This is just the kind of thing I'm talking about I triumphed. This will be an even split of the profits, fifty-fifty, right down the middle. I'm going to buy a little tape recorder and tape everything you say and then I'm going to write it down in a book of your gentle wisdom. You'll be famous, Dan Bee!

African Americans can now participate in the voting process Dan Bee replied. (I am paraphrasing.)

I am listening for the gentle wisdom in what you say for I know it is there old Dan Bee I emphasized. I know you don't mean it like it sounds. In our "politically correct" times, we are not used to the plainspoken ways of a more golden era of heavenly twilight memories of the "greatest generation." Perhaps, for example, you remember playing stickball with a ball and a stick. Or kicking the can in a carefree game of kick-the-can. Or riding on the hay in an old-fashioned hayride. Does that ring a bell, Dan Bee?

African Americans running the cannery reflected old Dan Bee. He went on to speculate on the effects of African American lifeguards who might breathe into the mouths of women who were not African Americans. Once again I paraphrase his salty usage of the regrettable vernacular of a bygone epoch. His hands were twitching upon the table in an agitated manner.

There there I soothed.

I reached for his hand and he grabbed mine tightly.

I have a fourth and final request I resumed. I would like to hire you as a private detective. I need you to follow this girl.

At this juncture I produced a photograph of my sister-in-law.

I've written down her name, her cell phone number and everything else I know about her. I don't have her exact address. That would be nice for a start! But I need all the information I can get. And lots of pictures. Do you have a spy camera of some kind, Dan Bee? I would imagine that you do. Maybe you could pretend to be dehydrated and knock on her door asking for water. If you could get into her bathroom I'd really appreciate some pictures of whatever she has in there. In her hamper and so forth. A picture or an actual item. Yes, an actual item. Something fairly small you could stuff in your pocket.

I saw with some relief that a fulsome amount of wisdom and canniness had sprung back forcefully into Dan Bee's eyes. He handled the photograph with heartening curiosity and verve.

Now this is her several years ago I cautioned. Back when she was still serious about her volleyball.

Can I keep this? Dan Bee requested.

Of course. I have several copies.

Makes my poor old wrung-out peter jump up stiff as a poker and almost as hot he related.

I beg your pardon old Dan Bee? I exclaimed.

He repeated his startling news in almost identical wording. Old Dan Bee then went on to spew forth a torrent of lascivious verbal pornography the likes of which America has never heard.

All the while my heart was breaking.

I presently perceived that old Dan Bee had reached through his open fly to dandle the venerated manhood swaddled therein.

This is indeed a tawdry and ruinous world was my conclusion.

Thereafter I was struck simultaneously by several epiphanies.

For one I realized that like all of us, old Dan Bee had good days and bad days, and that this was a bad day for old Dan Bee.

Chapter Twenty
Newberry's Historic Sutterfield Park

Newberry's historic Sutterfield Park is all that remains of the once wild forests of Newberry.

In its burgeoning days as a bustling settlement, unwelcome visitors often visited Newberry most unwelcomely from these neighboring forest regions!

Children were carried off by wolves, large cats and bears. Farmers were bitten by snakes and rats. Mosquitoes thrived in stagnant ponds. Hornet attacks were common. Rabid foxes caused consternation. A well-meaning naturalist imported scorpions. In retrospect, a poor decision.

Sutterfield Park also served as a blessed patch of green for many victims of Newberry's numerous public health tragedies. The dead and dying lay in great quantities expiring amidst the beauties of nature. Be it scarlet fever, diphtheria, typhoid or plain old mumps, no outbreak was too small, no epidemic too large to be accommodated by makeshift medical tents in Sutterfield Park.

These were just a few of the historical plaques I read while waiting for dusk. Why Newberry's historic Sutterfield Park was a veritable smorgasbord of historical plaques!

Eventually, however, I wearied of my researches, which had begun when I found that I had gotten to the park five hours earlier than intended. I suppose my excitement at the prospect of the "Haunted Ghost Walk Tour," which was to depart from the park's central fountain come sunset, was simply too much to bear! Also I was, technically, homeless. The Red Carpet Inn had refused to take cash for payment without an exorbitant deposit to back it up. And even when I had acquiesced to said deposit, it turned out that they could not accept it because my driver's license had expired, thus throwing my "identity" into question. Identity! Behold the frivolous frivolities of the modern age! Did General George Washington need a driver's license to stop at a friendly tavern for a tankard of grog? Even the Sproatsborough Strangler was welcomed into the homes of his victims with great cheer in those more innocent times of days of yore! This disreputable fellow was able to choke entire families with impunity thanks to the gentle and trusting ways of a more wondrous twilit era of old-fashioned values of neighborly good humor and "lending a helping hand."

I noted that I had received a painful and blistering sunburn due to my many hours in the park doing historical researches on the numerous plaques therein. I decided to phone my sister-in-law at once, thinking that she might spread healing ointments on the more tender portions of my being.

Sheila don't hang up! I cried. Something horrible has happened!

This better be good she sighed fetchingly.

I have a large and cumbersome brain tumor I explained. Doctors say it takes up almost the entire space of my inner skull. My actual brain has been scrunched up into the size of a sandwich.

Willie…

No, wait, I have to explain I thundered. The only reason I have been acting so strangely is because of my tumor. It presses on various nerves and blood vessels and so on and causes me to become erratic. I really want to apologize for the way I've acted toward you. It's the tumor's fault, Sheila! Can't we get together for a quiet dinner? I only have three weeks to live and I want to make it up to you. Medication is temporarily keeping my tumor under control so it should be a very nice dinner.

Willie I think we need to talk face to face. There are a couple of things I need to tell you she trilled.

I would like to buy you the most alluring steak in the world I proposed. I am at the park right now. I will hire a horse and carriage in which we will glide under the moon. Perhaps there are swans upon whom to gaze in the vicinity. Or water lilies!

That's not necessary she ululated lyrically.

I have recently come into a thousand dollars I impressed.

You say you're at the park? Can you meet me at the donut place across from the statue in half an hour? she panted.

Your wish is my command I pledged.

I hung up the phone with mixed feelings of alarm and delight. Perhaps, it occurred to me, my brain tumor theory was correct! It would explain so much. Certainly I was behaving like a man with a gigantic brain tumor. And once the tumor was removed my loved ones would gather around the bed and console me. We had you so wrong, Willie! All the time you were suffering while we heaped contumely upon you like a bunch of fiends!

Things were beginning to "turn around" for Willie Dobbs.

Chapter Twenty-one
A Fortune Made and Lost!

I entered a small, family-owned flower "shoppe" and ordered one thousand dollars worth of flowers.

Mister I ain't even sure we GOT a thousand dollars worth of flowers the amiable young florist protested.

Here is a thousand dollars cash I indicated. Get me as many flowers as you can. And with the remainder, if any, perhaps you will be so kind as to see to it that my order is delivered to yon donut shop as soon as possible.

Tomorrow? the florist guessed.

Within the half hour if possible I corrected.

Hell for a thousand dollars I'll start toting them over right now came the enthusiastic clarion call.

You will do no such thing! I reprimanded. They must look extremely gorgeous I rectified. I do not want a big mess of sloppy flowers.

I'm by myself here the florist acknowledged. I'll do my very best.

See that you do I commanded with a strutting air of *noblesse oblige*. With that I made my way to the donut shop.

Upon seating myself in a rather incommodious booth, it dawned upon me that I had been rather profligate with my nest egg, so soon after its auspicious receipt. Well, if there is one thing I have learnt from the study of history, it is that you cannot regret your actions of the past!

Order at the counter someone called from the counter.

I'm not ordering just yet I replied (conveniently neglecting to mention my recent and total lack of funds!).

Can't sit there without ordering came the rejoinder.

I'm meeting a friend I returned. A very special friend. Do you mind if I fill your establishment to the very rafters with exotic blossomings?

What are you talking about? was the understandable caveat.

Love, my good woman, love! Surely you have known the gentle touch of love! For this very evening I intend to ask for milady's hand in matrimony.

Good googly moogly! rang out the reply.

It has been my experience that even the swarthiest of entrepreneurs crumbles into a jelly of helpfulness when confronted by the stirrings of Monsieur Cupid! And so it was in this case. I remained undisturbed until a sinewy young woman in a sleeveless bowling shirt accosted me thusly:

Are you Willie Dobbs?

To which I replied in the positive.

She handed me a note—lavender paper in a lavender envelope—and was gone as quickly as she had come.

The contents of said note were distressing. It read:

Dear Willie,

I suppose I should thank you. Your persistent harassment has made me realize I should have come out to my family years ago. I am sure you will spread this around at once. It is something I should have taken care of myself. I am a lesbian. Even if I were not a lesbian I would not be attracted to you. Even if you were not married to my sister I would not be attracted to you. But I hope at least you will respect the fact that I am a lesbian and leave me alone. I am leaving soon for Alaska, as Amy has probably already told you. I will not be around a phone, so you will not be able to contact me for quite a long time. That is one of the most attractive aspects about moving to Alaska. I hope this separation will give you some time to cool off. I think you have a lot of problems and you should probably get some help. My girlfriend Sandy is trying to become a registered shaman. I have told her all about you and she agrees that you need help. For the next several months I will be finishing my dissertation on totem poles, while living among the people who make them. I hope you will make productive use of the time as well. You are a very sick man, Willie. I guess I feel bad for you more than anything. Please get help.

Sincerely,

Sheila

From the evidence of the crumpled missive clutched tenderly in my heartbroken fist as well as the salty tears of grief that had sprung with raging gusto into my jilted eyes, the large and understanding donut cashier intuited my situation.

She dumped you huh? was the gruff yet thoughtful assessment.

She has gone completely crazy I agreed. May I use your phone?

Is it a local call? the proprietress wondered.

Yes I lied.

For something at that moment made me realize something important about my wife. If I squinted she looked a lot like Sheila! Her figure was different, but by touching only certain parts of her during times of intimacy, my brain might be able to substitute the comforting if imaginary presence of Sheila. Fortunately, many of my wife's favorite activities of intimacy led to her face pointing in an outward direction from my own. Perhaps I could get her to grow her hair in a semblance of Sheila's! Nor was a wig out of the question for the purposes of a more immediate reconciliation. Most importantly I came to realize that I had only been in love with the IDEA of Sheila and not the actual Sheila, who was in fact a lesbian. Yet my wife and I shared a bond that only a husband and wife can share.

I sidled up to the counter and the donut lady pushed the phone toward me, along with an extra treat.

Here's a cruller and coffee she intimated. On the house.

Deep down inside people are good!

The call to my wife did not go well. First off, I was crying so much.

Somehow my wife got it into her head that I had found out about her affair with Carl Phipps, a big man at the chicken rendering plant. This was news to me! According to my wife, Carl Phipps was a man of large ambitions and expansive ideas, he was splitting off from the regular chicken rendering plant and starting his own chicken rendering plant, the world's first HUMANE chicken rendering plant, he had all kinds of blueprints drawn up about ways to make life better for chickens AND the people who kill the chickens. I was a little overawed by the amount of detail she was lavishing on me about the pipe dreams of Carl Phipps. She had never evinced half so much interest in food transport logistics! Or history! Though to be fair she had paid for my writing class. A meaningless but heartfelt gesture. Or was it merely a panacea for her guilty conscience? Or perhaps a ruse to get me "out of the way" so that she and Carl Phipps could enjoy their shenanigans freely?

The call ended badly.

I was briefly consoled by the realization of my cleverness: My father-in-law had "paid me off" for nothing. All along my wife had been planning to leave ME! I enjoyed the thought of the old crank "kicking himself" over his poor business dealings.

The donut lady seemed startled to see me weave so effortlessly between the polarities of weeping grievously and laughing riotously. Apparently her donut shop was not noted for the mental complexity of its customers! She asked me to leave several times.

It was at this juncture that the florist came in bearing armloads of flowers.

I'm calling this off I cautioned. Can I please have my thousand dollars back?

Are you expletive me? I've busted my expletive hump getting this organized. I've wrecked my expletive shop and ruined my flowers. He listed numerous other complaints, laced with expletives.

May I please have a partial refund? I suggested.

No he replied.

Chapter Twenty-two
The Strange Case of the Missing Ghost

I had burned all my bridges by painting myself into a corner and biting off more than I could chew. Like many American heroes throughout history I had become perhaps TOO ambitious. If it is a fault, it is an admirable one.

But one by one, fate had robbed me of my ambitions, leaving only one: buried treasure. This, I realized, had been my real goal all along.

As dusk began to fall about the donut shop I rushed for the central fountain in Sutterfield Park, hence to meet my destiny forthwith.

There they gathered in the gathering dark: knobkneed old tourists in their short pants and sandals with socks, standing alongside the large summer hats and hornrimmed glasses on beaded chains of their dumpling-shaped wives. Perhaps I am generalizing!

I was surprised to see that the "tour guide" was in fact a scrawny slip of a girl with frazzled red hair which frazzled forth surprisingly in many directions, like that of some sort of creature of the wild. I am not a zoologist! Suffice it to say she did not "look the part" of an experienced parapsychologist, and when she demanded my thirty dollars (which I did not have in any case) I determined to "grill" her on the subject of her expertise.

I trust you will be covering the famous ghosts of misers in the area I hinted.

We have a monk who hung himself in a belfry she babbled hopefully.

That is hardly a miser I reprimanded sternly.

Sir I believe you will enjoy the tour no matter what your ghostly preference. There are chills and spills galore she marketed cynically.

I get it! Put up or shut up. Is that your game? I prodded her.

Well sir, if you mean do you have to buy a ticket before you go on the chilling ghost walk of a lifetime, then yes sir, your answer is yes she admitted.

What qualifications do you have as a historian I demanded. I would like to see your Ph.D. certificate at once!

Sir I will have to ask you to get in the "spirit" of things she punned wretchedly.

Her coterie of yokels sniggered in amusement at the supposed waggery.

I shall report you to the National Board of Historians of which I am a prominent member I threatened. Now tell me about the creepy old miser!

Sir the ghost walk tour is for entertainment purposes only she claimed. Now if you would rather not purchase a ticket, that's up to you. But the rest of us need to be on our way. Very well. As you can see we are starting out here at the old fountain. This fountain was built in 1820. The architect was very famous in Europe and this was the first fountain he made in America. Unfortunately he was also known for his intensely jealous nature.

She went on to tell a very boring tale about an "Indian princess" who drowned in the fountain, perhaps as a suicide, perhaps by the hand of the very architect! And how the architect was cursed ever after and died of mysterious boils, crying her name.

I pointed out that her story was unsupported by historic fact.

The "tour guide" ignored me and began the "walking" part of the tour. I followed.

Sir I am going to have to ask you to leave our group she demanded irrationally.

The last time I checked America is a free country I countermanded patriotically. I happen to be taking a stroll. By coincidence my stroll happens to meander along the same environs as your beloved ghost walk… Or should I call it a "fake walk"? In any event, I fail to see why I should change my course merely because my chosen path of walking happens to coincide with yours.

Sir you are disrupting the fun of my group she speculated. It is my duty as their hostess to insure that they receive the good time they paid for. And you are making this very difficult.

Just ignore me I recommended.

Sir you did not pay for a ticket and I must once again ask you to leave she prattled.

Make me I challenged.

I don't make trash I burn it she taunted childishly.

Once more her feeble jape resulted in the untold merriment of her doddering charges.

I scooted toward her in what was apparently perceived as a threatening manner, waving my arms in a mock "fit," kicking up rocks and grass and making comical "ghost noises" which I intended as a lighthearted "icebreaker." I was more entertaining than she, you may be sure!

Several members of the tour group then held me to the ground and sat on me as the faux historian called 911 on that infernal modern gadget the cell phone.

Chapter Twenty-three
A Friend in High Places

My "booking" process was interrupted by a firm hand upon my shoulder. Even before turning I identified the possessor of said hand from his striking aftershave and virile grip. My blood seized up with terror and admiration.

I'll take this one Mitch. He's a pal. Say, be a sport and give him back his wallet.

It's empty anyway Mitch noted.

Hello buddy. Remember me? [Good Cop] asked.

His face was much the same: cocky, rugged, manly, square, fair-eyed, shrewd and—yes, in his peculiar way—decent.

How are you? I asked.

You stole my prowler. I had to call a friend for a lift. Very inconvenient.

That was quite a mix-up we had the other night I shrugged.

No hard feelings. We need to talk, Houdini. I'll pony up for some steak and eggs. How's that grab you?

I had no better offers. Indeed I was starved for both food and understanding.

Soon we were seated at a quaint diner, me, [Good Cop] and the scuffed satchel that now contained all my worldly goods. I ordered, as suggested, steak and eggs, the latter scrambled hard with cheddar cheese. [Good Cop] preferred his eggs "sunny side up," his yolks runny. He seemed in fact to relish their very sliminess. He sopped up the goo with rye toast, dry. I opted for the bran muffin. Though I still feared this man with all my heart, I could not help but appreciate the companionship and the marvelous stench of boiling hot black coffee which filled the very nostrils of the night.

I hate to bring this up I ventured. But the little movie critic? Is he doing better?

Who, him? Oh sure. We had a tea party and smoothed the whole thing over. We have a tea party every Sunday afternoon now, for we've become the bestest and jolliest of friends. Oh my goodness yes, now we just look back over the whole thing and laugh and laugh like a pair of idiots. It would fill your heart with joy to see the way we carry on.

I could barely hide my amusement at this charming admission, for [Good Cop] certainly did not seem to be the "tea party" type! He cut short my inner happiness with a stark query:

I hear tell you've been out to old Dan Bee's.

I dropped in on the old gent I conceded.

That's real keen of you. You ought to work for Meals on Wheels he suggested.

I really should take up some volunteer work I agreed. At this juncture I have virtually nothing left to do.

That's not what I hear. Old Dan Bee says you're talking up some scam. Low risk for high rollers.

Oh! I honestly didn't think I was getting through to him. Poor Dan Bee!

Poor Dan Bee nothing. He's got it on the ball, junior. Half the time, anyhow. Remember the other night when you were getting sexy in your shortie nightie?

I have no idea what you're talking about I blustered rightfully.

Sure you do. Angling to get a little spanky-panky from a defenseless old man? Running around and squealing all loosey goosey like? That's prime blackmail material, my friend. And me on the other side of the two-way mirror with the cutest little camcorder you ever saw. It's a hobby me and old Dan Bee do together, like dominoes.

First of all, old Dan Bee was only trying to cheer me up! Shame on you for misconstruing his intentions. Corporal punishment was the "norm" in his day and age. If people raised their children like old Dan Bee there would be a lot less crime. And second of all, I'm afraid you caught me on a bad day for blackmail. There's nobody left who cares.

All right, all right. Looking at you I can believe it. We'll play it your way for now. Then what's this scam old Dan Bee is rambling about?

I suppose he's referring to my buried treasure.

Treasure. You mean a score? Don't get coy with me. Spill.

Well if you're offering to chip in for the treasure hunt, you're more than welcome! The more the merrier! I have to admit, though, I'm beginning to think my prospects are pretty slim. Things were really looking up, you know? I made a cool grand just for leaving my wife. Can you believe that? Every man's dream, I guess. My father-in-law gave it to me because he hates me so much.

Oh yes, the famous father-in-law. He comes up a lot doesn't he? It's an "issue" for you. Goodness gracious. I can't see what he's got against a big brain like you.

Doesn't matter anyway. I blew the money. Every penny. Long story short, my day's been going downhill ever since. I got sunburned waiting for the "Historic Ghost Walk Tour." You ever heard of it?

[Good Cop] worked a toothpick.

Well, it's a gyp is what it is. I really ought to report them to the Better Business Bureau. I doubt they have a trained historian on the entire staff. I was hoping to get a bead on this treasure caper. There's supposed to be this wizened old miser in olden times who buried a treasure and now he's supposed to be a creepy old ghost with no tongue…

Stop it you're giving me the heebie jeebies. Now let's get back to the father-in-law for a minute. He rich, this father-in-law?

He drives a Lincoln Town Car.

Nice.

His toilets at his house are solid black. I mean solid black! They're SUPPOSED to be that way! The water faucets in the guest bathroom are pure gold.

Classy.

Sometimes I freeze up and I feel like I can't even pee. I don't care if I've had a whole pitcher of iced tea. Like his toilets are too good for me or something!

Heck, I don't know, partner [Good Cop] comforted. Seems like to me he's selling you short. This is just as an outside observer, you understand. I bet he could afford more than a thousand, easy. A thousand that's already history, by the way. There's plenty more where that came from, I bet. Way I see it you're entitled, everything you put up with. I say we put the squeeze on him. Tell him you're coming back to your sweet Betsy Lee unless he forks over ten more g's. Make that fifty g's.

Wow! This is the finest plan I have ever heard I gushed. We should implement it right away before he finds out my wife left me for that Carl

Phipps.

Oh, we'll implement it all right. And if he says no I'll notch his ears.

I'm not familiar with the term I expressed.

I'll put a little notch in his ear with my little knifey.

Oh, notching his ears! Fantastic. Well, what are we waiting for?

We hurried to [Good Cop]'s car, a vintage 1978 Oldsmobile Cutlass Supreme, white, with a white vinyl top.

It even had a working 8-track player!

This reminds me of historical times I commented.

We enjoyed an 8-track tape recording of Paul Simon's historic *One Trick Pony* album as we sped into the night.

Chapter Twenty-four
Boyle County's Famous "Bog Country"

We were in the midst of a most amiable agreement that Dabney Coleman is a highly underrated actor when I began to question where exactly we were.

Dark isn't it? summarized my new "business partner."

Extremely I seconded.

No lights out here he explained. You never been to bog country?

Shamefully not, but I've read a great deal about it in my researches I assured him. Perhaps we'll see one of its famous "will-o-the-wisps"!

Yeah, wouldn't that just be the bee's knees?

But if I recall accurately, this is taking us quite a bit north of South Preston. You really should have let me help more with the directions! I chided.

I know just where I'm going he contradicted. Whenever I have a problem I just mosey out to these bogs.

And your problems just sink away I smiled.

Something like that.

[Good Cop] stopped the car.

I sense an epiphany coming on! I encouraged him brightly.

Try this one on for size he returned. I don't really need you for this shakedown. I just need the idea of you. Is that an epiphany?

Yes and a very metaphysical one at that! I chirped agreeably. In my estimation you are the ideal Emersonian man! Did you ever read his essay on self-reliance?

I wrote the book on self-reliance, junior. Guy like you gums all that up. Look at you. You're bad luck.

You've certainly got my number! I confessed.

The good news is, your bad luck just ran out.

Great! I cheered.

The bad news is, ALL your luck just ran out he finished.

You lost me I replied.

That's the idea. Out of the car.

But this is the deadly bog country I reminded him.

He touched his finger to his nose in an effort to tell me nonverbally that I had guessed his intention "on the nose."

Quite a vigorous tussle ensued!

Perhaps my emotions had been "bottled up" for too long! Perhaps another betrayal was just too many for one day! In any case, before I knew what was happening I found that I had shoved him halfway out of his side of the car and was banging his head repeatedly upon the narrow roadway. He broke loose and rolled into the street, reaching for his gun even as he rolled, in an impressive display of the acuity of his professional training. With superhuman instinct, however, I jumped on top of him, knocking the weapon from his hand and into the dreaded bog. He leapt to his feet and lunged after his cherished murder weapon, realizing his mistake too late.

Help! Help! he suggested repeatedly.

At this juncture my thoughts were exhausted and confused and I am afraid I could offer but little aid beyond the occasional word of encouragement until his head disappeared from view. It seemed as if even the headlights' faithful gleam was being sucked into the eternalness of the black bog. That detail is for you, Mr. Writing Instructor!

My emotions were mixed. Overall, however, it gave me a warm sense of satisfaction to sit and picture [Good Cop] there at the bottom of the bog, pickled in perfect historical condition for some enterprising Willie Dobbs type of 10,000 years in the future. He who in life had done so much harm would in death become a wondrous boon for scholarly researches! Much like that fellow who was preserved in Ireland. I believe his name was "The Piltdown Man" though at this juncture I no longer have access to the library.

Chapter Twenty-five
A New Beginning!

Sometimes the treasure we are seeking is not the one we find! Is THIS the mysterious secret after all? Is THIS, perhaps, the mysterious secret of the valuable treasure? Yes! Apparently it is! Isn't that interesting? The whole time you think the treasure is one thing but then it turns out to be another thing. Weird!

Take me, for example. I ended up not with rubies and pearls, but with the rather more prosaic reward of an Oldsmobile Cutlass Supreme, the trunk of which yielded untold riches of yet a different sort! Some dynamite, various automatic weapons, a cattle prod, a machete, brass knuckles, a brickbat, a box of hand grenades, what I believe to be cocaine or heroin in sacks (or possibly plastic explosives) a briefcase full of hundred dollar bills and several credit cards in various names. Tonight, by way of example, I am registered as Bertram Green in a very nice hotel in St. Louis, Missouri, home of the historical St. Louis Arch, which is viewable even now through my impressive window.

Have I become then the epitome of modernistic modern man, rootless, shiftless, devoid of real identity? Such was my initial fear!

But think of it this way: Am I not, rather, the very semblance of the original pioneers? Striking out with little more than the clothing on their backs! Blazoning the trails of civilization upon the beleaguered yokes of thrusting oxen. Going forth at the command of the very wind itself, blowing hither and yon across the plains of this great nation toward some ultimate destiny of unimaginable import. Yes, in answer to your question, that is exactly what I am like.

In my case, the voices of fate seem to be leading me toward Washington, D.C., our nation's historic capital. My purpose there—still misty to me for the nonce—is in any case beyond the provenance of the present trifle! Indeed I now must regrettably close this current volume, as the time has come for me to stop writing with a pencil or a keypad and to use something more substantial: Lightning—or blood!—might make an appropriate metaphor as the "writing" tool in question! In any case, this new form of history will be "read" in the icy tundra of far Alaska and in the humbler reaches of dear South Preston as well. The country club will be abuzz with the news. My father-in-law shall keel over in his golf cart, perhaps falling off and allowing said golf cart to run over his fragile neck, twisting his head all the way around on his body in a final grimace of despair and making an open casket out of the question. Carl Phipps himself shall make dookey in his pants, perhaps as he addresses the Chamber of Commerce in front of all his friends. In short, the number is literally numberless of persons who will sit up and take note, exclaiming Wow! I guess Willie Dobbs had more "gumption" than we thought! Thank you for putting us "on the map," Willie Dobbs! And a notable figure will at last arise to chime forth South Preston's name like a mighty chime chiming forth.

In closing, do I have any advice for aspiring scribes? You bet I do! Don't let "the turkeys" get you down! Everything happens for a reason! Writing is fun—and easy! People need—nay, hunger!—to enjoy your masterful descriptions of chipmunks and faculty dinners and enchanted hobgoblins and Eastern European discotheques and trees! And so forth! So do "what you have to do" and reach for your dreams! Believe in yourself! Only YOU will know when it is time to stop writing and get a real job. Like me.

ABOUT THE CONTRIBUTORS

HAVEN BROWN received his MFA from the world-renowned Ogden Institute. His works have appeared or are forthcoming in *Wadded Leaves*, *Spoonbender*, *The Tallapoosa Review*, *Squanto!* and other, less well-known, publications. He lives in rural Pennsylvania with his wife Debbie, an amateur cigar-roller.

EUGENIA EUGENIA has published two hundred and forty volumes of poetry. Her work has appeared in a million literary journals and forty-six thousand anthologies, including *Pardon my Nuts* and *Kitty-Cats are Coming*.

HARVEY PINCHMAN lives in New York and Paris and Northern Alabama, where he is a tenant farmer. *My Corns Hurt!*, a humorous memoir of his experiences in Paris, will be published by Angry Duck Press shortly after his upcoming death.

ROGER RAVEN's first novel, *Here Falleth Thine Eyes*, won the Goalsetter's Prize for Advances in Punctuation. His second novel, *Be Thou the Dawn*, was nominated for an honorable mention citation by the American Association of Fiction with Recipes In It. He is also the recipient of the Robert Grouse Foundation Grant of Money for Poor People and a "silver level" member of the Hertz Rent-a-Car Special Bonus Circle. He is at work on a third novel, as yet untitled.

CHUCK RINDEL lives in Warm Springs, Georgia, where he has full custody of his three beautiful children, Molly, Evan and Dylan. He would kill to protect them. If somebody sets foot on somebody else's property without permission, that is called trespassing, and it is 100% legal to kill that person.

HAMILTON RUTTS is a lifelong native of Ames, Iowa. After 30 years as a practicing drywall installer, Rutts retired to pursue his dream of writing. "Thoughts on Jackin' Off" is his first published work.

ALTHEA SANDS is author of the chapbook *My Father's Apples* and the microbook *The Way of the Kite*, which can only be read with a microscope. Her poems have appeared in *Totem: The Magazine of Totems*, *Wrinkled Raisin* and elsewhere.

SHELLEY SAUNDERS is a recent graduate of the Peach Melba Writer's Workshop, where she was awarded a "Hoops" Baxter Senior Fellowship in Fantastic Writing. Her calendar *Baby Zoo Animals* was chosen by Flip Hawkins for publication by the Calendar Club.

BOB SEARS writes nutty, cavalier contributor's notes about himself to show that he doesn't take the whole thing too seriously. Sometimes he writes something like, "**BOB SEARS** enjoys in-line skating, surfing and hitting his own thumb with a hammer." Hilarious! His cheeky blurbs about himself have appeared in *Hoecake*, *The Bent River Review* and *The Oscar Homulka Quarterly*.

SKIP SHELL is a painter, cook and raconteur. When not traveling the world in his nicely painted convertible, Skip amuses himself by pulling the wings off flies.

GRETCHEN TIFFLER draws on her experience as a Girl Scout leader to write realistic stories of hiking. She is married to Horace Weems, a renowned tuba player.

WALLACE TROT is just about the cutest thing ever. The things he writes make people wet their pants. His accomplishments, literary and otherwise, are so numerous and varied as to boggle the mind, and as such will not be listed here or, indeed, anywhere.

MARTIN "SPRAIN" TURNER translates other people's poetry into Russian then gets someone else to translate it back into English. He then translates *that* back into Russian and gets someone *else* to translate the result into German. And then he translates *that* into English and puts his name on it. He is the author of *The Rime of the Ancient Mariner* by Samuel

Taylor Coleridge and a whole book of poems by Philip Larkin.

TIMOTHY VALE shares his spacious Cape Cod home with the light of his life, a rather quarrelsome budgie named Herodotus.